MIDWINTER
BURNING

MIDWINTER BURNING

TANYA LANDMAN

WALKER
BOOKS

First published 2022 by Walker Books Ltd
87 Vauxhall Walk, London SE11 5HJ

Text © 2022 Tanya Landman
Cover and interior illustrations © 2022 Tom Clohosy Cole

This book has been typeset in ITC Leawood and Humana

Printed and bound by CPI Group (UK) Ltd, Croydon CR0 4YY

British Library Cataloguing in Publication Data:
a catalogue record for this book is available from the British Library

ISBN 978-1-4063-9718-5

www.walker.co.uk

FSC
www.fsc.org

MIX
Paper from
responsible sources
FSC® C171272

For Raffy

PART 1

The stone circle – temple of the Goddess, Mother Earth – was at last complete. It had taken many, many, moons but now the labour was done. The Seer stood at its sacred heart, the only member of the clan permitted to set foot on hallowed ground. Stretching out arms that were wrinkled and slack with age, she tipped her head back and uttered a prayer of thanks to Mother Earth.

The Goddess had been generous this past year. She had given freely and the whole clan had thrived. Even Smidge, the foundling, was content.

Smidge... Why did he come to mind now, when the Seer was at prayer? Such a lonely little lad! So different from the rest of the clan, with his flame-red hair and green eyes. And such a dreamer! She had found him on the beach ten summers before, a baby, bound into a floating basket, and assumed he was the child of traders from across the sea.

Abandoned?

Perhaps.

Or the sole survivor of a shipwreck, saved from the storm by the hand of the Goddess? That was possible too.

The questions that had arisen when she'd first laid eyes on the baby were still unanswered.

Was he a blessing or a curse?

A gift from the Goddess?

Or a trick, played by a demon?

The clan had debated long and hard about whether they should keep him or kill him. Kindness had prevailed in the end, but in truth Starver still doubted the wisdom of that decision. And there were many who agreed with him.

Yet for now there were more important things for the Seer to think about. Mother Earth's divine generosity did not come without a price.

At Midwinter, at the turning of the year, there would be a feast. And there would be a sacrifice. She would know the victim soon enough. The Goddess would send a vision. A sign. Whatever She required would be done. Come what may, Mother Earth must be repaid for Her generosity.

With blood.

1939

FRIDAY 1 SEPTEMBER

LEAVING LONDON

He was Mum's little accident. Spilled milk, she called him. Not worth crying over.

So she didn't. Other mothers were clinging to their offspring as they assembled in the playground at six o'clock that morning. Children stood dazed, still half asleep, luggage labels tied to their buttonholes, gas masks dangling around their necks, bulging rucksacks fixed on their backs. Some were so weighty they looked as though they might pull their owners over.

Alfie hovered uncertainly at the edge of the crowd as he always did. Mum, who liked to be at the heart of things, frowned at him in irritation.

They didn't have a rucksack at home, so Alfie carried a cardboard suitcase that was almost as big as he was. All it contained were spare socks and an extra set of underclothes, a pair of pyjamas, a toothbrush, a torn piece of towel that would serve as a flannel, and a jam sandwich for the journey. The children were allowed to take just one toy with them. Some clutched dolls or teddy bears tightly to their chests. Alfie's most precious possession was a magnifying glass that had long ago lost both frame and handle. The chipped, circular slab of domed glass was tucked safely into the pocket of his shorts, the weight of it strangely reassuring. He'd outgrown his coat, and Mum hadn't yet bought him a replacement so she tied his label around his neck on a long length of string. It flapped in his face, teasing him just like Billy Figgs and his gang.

Alfie Wright! Alfie Right? Alfie Wrong, more like!

The kids on his street jeered whenever they saw him coming. And yet, to begin with, the only real difference between Alfie and Billy and the others was that they had fathers who'd married their mothers. Even if some of those dads hadn't stayed around to see their children growing up, they still had names and faces and histories that their offspring could boast about. All Alfie had was a big, empty space. His mother wouldn't or couldn't say who his father was, and that had been enough to mark him out. But Alfie was also a dreamer and a loner, who liked his own company. Harmless enough differences, to be sure, but on Alfie's street being different – for whatever reason – was never good.

Go away! Get lost! You ain't wanted 'ere!

It was true. Nobody *did* want him. Not even his mum. He'd told her about their teasing – just once – and she'd sighed wearily and said, "You've got to fight your own battles, Alfie. I can't do it for you."

And now Germany had invaded Poland. Alfie suspected that the war, which everyone said would start any day now, was a welcome relief to his mother. The evacuation was a convenient excuse. She could do what she'd always wanted and pack him off like a parcel, send him away to strangers. As soon as he was out of sight, she'd forget about him. With Alfie gone, she'd be able to go dancing with "the girls" – women who worked in the same factory as her – whenever she fancied. She could stay out all night if she wanted to. Her foot was already tapping out a rhythm on the ground.

"Off you go, Alf," she said, nodding towards the other children. A polished fingernail stabbed him in the back. He turned, half hoping to see tears trickling over her cheeks, but her cold, grey eyes slid down his face like rainwater off a lump of lard.

"You be a good boy now. Don't go giving no one no trouble, you hear me?"

She didn't even wait to watch the assembled children leave. There was no tear-stained handkerchief bravely raised in the air as they set off for the station. By the time they reached the end of the street and Alfie looked back over his shoulder, Mum had gone.

GOODBYE, MR MOORE

Mr Moore was standing on his one leg at the corner of the street, wobbling a little unsteadily on his crutches. As the line of children progressed along the pavement towards him, Alfie saw that two steady streams of tears were running down the old man's face, cutting a line of white across his grubby cheeks.

According to Mum, Mr Moore had lost half his left leg and all of his mind in the last war. The things he'd seen in the trenches had turned his brain inside out, she said. He was haunted by ghosts. That was why he was always having conversations with people that weren't there.

"Best to keep away from him, Alf," Mum had told him. "A man like that? You never know what he might do."

That was easier said than done. One day last summer, Alfie had come home from school to find Mr Moore sitting on their front doorstep like an empty milk bottle. Alfie couldn't get past him, so, instead, he'd sat down next to the muttering old man and waited for Mum to finish her shift. Alfie hadn't much minded. The day was warm and he'd done what he always did when there was nothing else to do. Pulling the magnifying glass from his pocket, and shutting his right eye, he held it up so close to his left that Mr Moore, the whole street and everything in it blurred and smudged out of focus. With his magnifying glass, Alfie could make the rest of the world simply go away for a while. He'd fall into a sort of daydream, watching vague, fuzzy scenes playing out in front of him as if he was in his own, private cinema.

As Mr Moore talked to his imaginary friends, Alfie could see them taking shape. Indistinct, insubstantial shadows, like reflections in a shop window, of two young men dressed in uniform, standing either side of Mr Moore, chatting with him.

"It will all be over by Christmas, they said. They were having a laugh, weren't they, Eric?" said the first with a grin.

"The joke was on us right enough, Bob," agreed the second.

"Come on, lads. Be fair," said Mr Moore with a wink. "They never said *which* Christmas, did they?"

All three of them erupted into laughter, the two young men's hearty chuckles followed by Mr Moore's soft, wheezy splutter that ended in a cough.

They were nice company, Alfie thought. He had been perfectly content sitting in the sunshine with Mr Moore and his friends until Billy Figgs had come along.

How long the older boy had been standing there watching them Alfie couldn't be sure. He felt a sudden kick in his side, so hard and sharp he dropped his magnifying glass. He hurtled back into the real world with such speed that, for a moment, he felt breathless and dizzy. The two young men had vanished. There was just him and Mr Moore, who was mumbling to himself like a madman.

"Don't they make a lovely couple?" mocked Billy. He was looking at Alfie and Mr Moore but he was talking to Ned Smith and Stan Murphy, who were in the same class as Alfie at school. Violet Davies and the other kids stood behind them, and they all cackled with laughter.

Mr Moore pulled himself upright and lurched off down the road, still mumbling. Billy headed after him with a grin, mimicking the old man's uneven gait and wild, staring eyes. "Who are you talking to, Mr Moore? You know there ain't no one there, don't you?"

The other children followed as if Billy Figgs was a kind of modern-day Pied Piper. Now able to get to the front door, Alfie stood up and went inside. So he didn't see Violet glancing back at him with a faintly guilty, apologetic expression on her face.

It wasn't just Billy who was unkind to Mr Moore. Grown-ups looked at the old man as if he didn't belong. Not belonging was so familiar to Alfie that he always felt a kind of kinship with the former soldier. Mum said that now another war was about to start, Mr Moore's last remaining shreds of sanity had been blown to the wind. He should be locked up, she said. Alfie had heard her and the neighbours muttering together. "He isn't safe," they told each other. "He should be put in the loony bin. For his sake and for everyone else's."

And now, as the children trooped along the street towards the railway station in the dawn light, they all gave Mr Moore a wide berth as if he was a human bomb that might explode in their faces.

Alfie didn't move out of the way. Nearing the old man, he could hear him softly pleading, protesting to an invisible person standing somewhere to the left of him. "They're children. They're younger than we were! They can't take the children away. Where are they going? It's ain't right!"

"Goodbye, Mr Moore," Alfie said, stopping for a moment in front of the old man. "Don't worry about us."

Mr Moore ignored him and carried on with his conversation. "They can't send children to fight. They mustn't go."

"It's all right, Mr Moore. We ain't fighting or nothing. They're sending us off to the countryside. To keep us safe."

That one word seemed to penetrate Mr Moore's fog. "Safe?" he echoed. It was as if he didn't know the meaning of the word.

"Safe," Alfie repeated. "Don't worry. We'll be safe."

"Nowhere's safe!" Mr Moore told the invisible person beside him. "It's lies. All lies."

Alfie put his hand on the old man's arm, giving it a reassuring squeeze. "They said it will be like a holiday. They're evacuating us. We'll be all right."

It took Mr Moore some time but at last he focussed on the living, breathing boy standing in front of him. He looked down at the fingers squeezing his arm, then reached out his own hand and touched Alfie on the cheek.

"You won't be," he said.

Alfie didn't know how to reply. And, in any case, there was no time to say more. The line of children was rapidly disappearing down the road and Alfie had to run to catch up with them, which was no mean feat with the gas mask banging against his chest and the suitcase bashing into his legs. He heard Mr Moore calling after him, "You won't be safe!"

Alfie felt a prickle of alarm but told himself sternly that Mr Moore wasn't right in the head. The old man might be haunted by ghosts of the past, but he couldn't possibly see into the future.

Could he?

ARRIVING

Alfie had never been on a train before. He'd never even set foot outside his tiny corner of London. And now there were so many people crammed together into one place. Every child in the city – no, every child in the whole, wide world! – seemed to be in the station. The air was thick with soot and steam and sweat. Grown-ups with clipboards yelled their heads off, shrieking out names of schools and their destinations.

"Platform Nine, children!" Miss Bottomley, the young teacher in charge of Alfie's group, shouted, struggling to make herself heard. "This way. Follow me!"

Terrified of getting lost, of being left behind or drowning in the sea of humanity, Alfie grabbed the belt of Miss Bottomley's coat in his left hand. Though she tried to bat him away, Alfie didn't let go.

Keeping tight hold of his suitcase in his other hand, he stumbled awkwardly behind her as she pushed her way through to Platform Seven.

Things were no easier when they reached the train. They had to cram themselves in like tinned sardines and there were no seats left in any of the carriages. Miss Bottomley had to stand and Alfie ended up perched on his suitcase in the corridor.

He barely had time to catch his breath before the engine whistled and started puffing its way out of the station, billowing clouds of steam into the choked city air.

As soon as the train was moving, Alfie started to feel something strange and unexpected. All around him, white-faced children were trying – and failing – to be the brave little soldiers their parents had urged them to be.

"It's a tremendous adventure, children," Miss Bottomley declared, desperately trying to jolly them along. "It will be like the most wonderful holiday. We're going to have a thoroughly splendid time."

She repeated it over and over, as if, by saying the words often enough, they'd magically become true, but some of Alfie's classmates were already crying for their mothers. Violet Davies' little brother Jack was wailing so loudly he gave himself hiccups and there was nothing Violet could do to make them stop. Even Miss Bottomley, who must have been at least twenty years old, was looking like she might burst into tears at any moment.

Yet Alfie felt peculiarly light-headed. Something was swelling in his chest like a balloon, rising up onto his face, curling his lips into a broad smile.

"What you grinning at?" said Billy, whose jaw was clenched with the effort of holding in his tears.

Alfie didn't answer. He couldn't. Because what *was* this sensation coursing through his veins? It was so unfamiliar he couldn't put a name to it, not until the train jolted as it passed over the points, and he banged his shoulder hard against the window.

It was then that Alfie realized he was feeling happy.

They travelled all day, changing trains in two big cities that Alfie couldn't remember the names of. It was mid-afternoon when they boarded a third train, which rattled and clacked along a winding track between rolling hills, past lushly green fields and then beside a bright, sparkling river, so unlike the grey-green Thames that Alfie wasn't sure it was even the same thing. Each time they stopped, the vast throng of children that had boarded their train in London diminished. Names of schools were shouted out at each station and children disembarked onto the platform, clumping together like anxious sheep before being herded away. And then the train moved on again, growing emptier and emptier with each stop until it reached the end of the line. There, half the remaining children, including Ned Smith and Stan Murphy – Billy Figgs' most loyal and devoted friends – were led towards a village hall to be claimed by their host families. Billy stared after them. He looked smaller all of a sudden, Alfie thought. And scared.

The dozen children left in Miss Bottomley's care had to board a little bus that sputtered up hills and down into valleys along lanes that twisted and turned so much everyone turned a pale shade of green. Billy was the first to be sick, and, after that, it was like a game of follow-my-leader. The bus had to keep stopping as children heaved up whatever their parents had packed for their lunch. Poor Miss Bottomley was doing her best to soothe them and, before long, her shoes and coat were spattered with flecks of vomit. Alfie was the only one who didn't feel ill. Ignoring the chaos on the bus, he stared out of the window in mesmerized delight as the landscape unfolded around him.

At last, the sick, subdued little group of children and the weary young teacher reached a village that nestled at the foot of a wooded hillside.

The bus pulled up in a tiny square, stopping outside a one-roomed school building that stood next to the church. Two savage-looking, wolf-like dogs were tied up outside and started to growl menacingly as the children disembarked.

"Down, Rex! Down, Sheba!" snapped a voice. The dogs dropped to their bellies instantly. The middle-aged woman who had given the command now turned her attention to the new arrivals. Tutting crossly and peering down her beak-like nose at Miss Bottomley, the woman barked, "You're very late! Wherever have you all been? I was almost ready to give up on you!"

She glared accusingly at the tired teacher as if Miss Bottomley was personally responsible for the slow-running trains and the winding lanes and the children's travel sickness.

The woman didn't seem to expect a reply. She carried on, "Look lively, there. Come on, step inside. We haven't got all day. Lady Atherington," she said, grasping Miss Bottomley's hand and giving it a cursory shake. "And you're in charge, I take it. Name?"

"Miss Bottomley."

"Well, Miss Bottomley, you shall be coming with me later. I've arranged an attic room at the Manor to be cleared for your use. I trust you'll find it satisfactory.

Let's get these children disposed of first, though, shall we?"

Lady Atherington was all angles, Alfie thought, as she ushered them into the schoolroom. It was as if she'd been drawn by someone who'd only been allowed to use straight lines. She wore a navy skirt and matching jacket that looked almost military. Broad-shouldered and wide-hipped, her body was pinched in so tightly at the waist that her two halves looked like triangles, one set upside down on top of the other. Her hat was adorned with long, narrow feathers, which seemed to have been fired into it like arrows, and her mouth was a violent red streak across her face. Alfie knew it was lipstick. It was the same shade his mother wore, but, whereas she made it look glamorous, on Lady Atherington it looked alarmingly like blood.

They were all given a glass of squash and a biscuit. And then Lady Atherington made the children line up like soldiers on parade, displaying them for the grown-ups to pick and choose.

A nursery rhyme ran through Alfie's head as he waited.

Five currant buns in a baker's shop,
Round and fat with sugar on the top.
Along came a boy with a penny one day,

Bought a currant bun and took it away.
Four currant buns...

One by one the children disappeared with host families, looking relieved or apprehensive depending on who had picked them out. Billy Figgs, being tall for his age and strong, was chosen by a man who Alfie later discovered was the landlord of the village pub. He came in smelling of beer and tobacco and announced he wanted "a lad to help with the deliveries". Carrie and Claire Thompson, the identical twins in the year below Alfie at school, were led away by a young woman with a crying baby of her own perched on one hip. Violet Davies and her brother Jack were selected by two elderly women, who loudly declared as they departed that children should be seen and not heard. At last, of the dozen evacuees, only Alfie was left, standing alone in the middle of the schoolroom.

Yet, somehow, despite the awkwardness of the situation, despite the looks that the two women took turns to dart at him – anxious in Miss Bottomley's case, irritated in Lady Atherington's – the bubble of happiness that had taken up residence in Alfie's chest still didn't burst. He felt a strange, unshakeable certainty that someone was coming for him. They might be taking an awful long time, but Alfie knew they'd get here in the end. He just had to amuse himself until then, that was all. And amusing himself was something Alfie was an expert at.

He pulled the magnifying glass from his pocket and held it up to his eye so that the world blurred and smudged. He could watch the vague, fuzzy scenes playing out in front of him for hours.

Yet today something different happened.

He knew that he was still in the schoolroom. He could hear Lady Atherington interrogating Miss Bottomley about her family background. Behind him, a fly was banging itself against the windowpane. Someone in the lane outside called a greeting to someone else. A dog barked.

But through the magnifying glass, the world, instead of blurring, became crystal clear. Where there had been schoolroom walls only a second before, there were now trees.

He turned full circle. He seemed to be standing in a small clearing. Birdsong pierced his ears. When he looked up, instead of a timbered ceiling, there were fragments of blue sky through interlaced branches. Although it was September, the leaves were just beginning to come out, pinpricks of vividly bright green bursting from buds. A breeze stirred spiral ferns uncurling between mossy tree roots. The ground was carpeted with flowers that were a deeper and richer blue than the sky. Alfie breathed in their sweet scent, all mixed up with damp moss and rich earth, and was almost dizzied by it. And then there was a rustling to his left, a stirring in the undergrowth, an animal smell.

Something was coming towards him.

Something big.

HELLO, AUNTIE BELL

Bang! The sudden noise jerked Alfie back into the schoolroom.

The door had crashed open. Alfie stood blinking, feeling dazed and confused. Usually, the scenes he saw with his magnifying glass were indistinct, but the woodland had been clear, solid and real, and the animal smell still lingered in his nostrils.

A woman with an almost perfectly round face and apple-red cheeks came in. If Lady Atherington had been drawn with straight lines, this woman had been drawn in nothing but curves. She stood for a moment, looking around the almost-empty schoolroom.

"I'm so sorry I'm late, Lady Atherington," she said in a warm, mellow voice. She had an accent that was unfamiliar to Alfie, but instantly appealing. "Ted was going to let me have the cart but then Blossom lost a shoe. I could have taken Makepeace, I suppose, but I can't always manage him on my own. So I had to walk. I don't want to be having any accidents with the cart, do I? Not when I'm meant to be looking after a poor little evacuee. Wherever are they all? Have they gone?"

Her eyes scanned the room as if evacuees might peek out from behind curtains or emerge from under the floorboards. And then her gaze came to rest on Alfie.

There was a pause as she looked him up and down. And then she said, "Oh, my dear! Are you the very last one?"

She walked over and stood before him. Then – with visible effort and loudly creaking knees – she bent down so her eyes were level with his.

She smiled, a grin so broad it seemed to crack her face in two.

"Saved the best for last, I see, Lady Atherington. Thank you kindly. A nice tidy lad to come live with me and Ted. That's my son," she explained to Alfie. "He's a big grown-up man now, mind, but he's still my baby. You're exactly what I was hoping for. A little lad to make a fuss of. I'm Mrs Hartland, but you can call me by my first name if you like. Mind you, it's a bit of a mouthful. Dowsabel. Have you ever heard the like? I don't know what Mother and Father were thinking, naming me that. More a name for a cow than a woman, my husband Bill always said. He just called me Bell. Bill and Bell we were, while he was alive, chiming together in perfect harmony. He passed away ten years or more ago now, God rest his soul, and, since then, I've been chiming alone, you might say. But we've got to make the best of things, haven't we? I dare say I'll be seeing him again in heaven, when the time comes. How about you call me Bell, like Bill did? Auntie Bell? Would that suit you?"

Alfie didn't seem to be required to speak. He nodded mutely and the flow of her talk carried on.

"And what's your name, my birdie? Oh, I can read it on your label. Let's take that thing off, shall we? Makes you look like a parcel. Alfie Wright? Well, Alfie, right you most certainly are. It's very nice to meet you, young man. Say goodbye to your teacher now, and then you can come along with me and we'll get you settled into your new home."

THE LONG WALK HOME

"I hope you don't mind a bit of a walk, Alfie dear," Auntie Bell said. "I know tis getting late in the day but if we keep up a steady pace we should get there before dark."

She braced her knees and bent to pick up his suitcase. It was a huge thing, big enough for Alfie to curl up and go to sleep in if he'd wanted to. Before Alfie could tell Auntie Bell that it was almost empty, she'd heaved it off the ground. Finding it unexpectedly light, she accidentally swung it so high in the air that she lost her balance and toppled sideways into Lady Atherington.

There was a bit of a kerfuffle as the two women extricated themselves, during which Lady Atherington's feather-spiked hat got knocked off her head. Auntie Bell apologized profusely but, as soon as she and Alfie were out of the schoolroom and had edged carefully past the two snarling dogs that were tied up outside, she started giggling.

"Oh my Lord! Did you see the look on Her Ladyship's face? Thought I was going to squash her flat, I expect. And her blessed hat!"

She laughed until the tears were rolling down her face. Alfie wasn't used to grown-ups sharing a joke with him and didn't quite know how to react. It was nice, he decided finally, even if it was a surprise. He gave Auntie Bell a tentative smile.

"Silly me!" Auntie Bell said, as soon as she could draw breath. "Daft old baggage, I am. Come on, Alfie Wright. Let's be on our way. We'll go by the lane, I think. Tis quicker to take the path along the valley but tis muddy at the moment and those shoes of yours don't look quite up to the job."

As they progressed through the village, Auntie Bell greeted everyone they saw. "Evening, Mrs Peterson! How's your hip? Sorry to hear that. Hello, Mrs Copper! Nice weather for the time of year, isn't it?"

The other woman sniffed and said gloomily, "We shall have rain tomorrow."

Under her breath, Auntie Bell said to Alfie, "She's a miserable one! Never anything cheerful to say. Mind you, her husband's dead and she has her father-in-law to look after and he's as sour as they come! I dare say it has to rub off somewhere along the line. Best avoid them both, if you can."

As they passed the smithy, she called, "Afternoon, George! Blossom's cast a shoe. When shall I bring her in?"

"Can't do nothing until next week," the man replied. "Got a job on for Her Ladyship and you know how particular she is. Shall we say Wednesday morning? Bring Blossom in then and I'll see her right."

"Will do."

There were just a few more houses, strung out along the lane like beads on a necklace, and then they were walking over a bridge and out of the village.

On the other side of the bridge, there was a fork in the road.

Auntie Bell pointed to the right. "That leads to Atherington Manor. Don't ever go down there unless you're expressly invited. Her Ladyship does not take kindly to trespassers. Poachers, she calls them. Though why she thinks anyone would be thieving rabbits from her land when they're running free all over the cliffs is anyone's guess. You saw those dogs of hers tied up outside the school? Nasty things. She lets them run loose in the grounds and you don't want to go meeting them when they're off the lead." She heaved a sigh. "Tis a pity, really. It was different when her husband was alive … but that's a long time ago. He was killed in the last war and now her son's gone off to fight in this one. She's got her reasons for being spiky, I dare say. Tis a terrible shame, though. When His Lordship was alive, he used to allow the whole village to cross his land come the Midwinter Burning. Tis the most direct path to the stones, see? And Lord Atherington always led the procession himself, no matter what the vicar said."

Alfie had no idea what she was talking about, and the puzzlement must have shown on his face because she continued, "Midwinter Burning? You'll be wondering what that is, of course! Tis a bit of nonsense, really. An old tradition around these parts. I don't know who started it or when – tis buried in the mists of time, as they say. The vicar doesn't much approve of it, mind. He says tis an old heathen thing that should be consigned to the dustbin, but there isn't no one who listens to that. The Midwinter Burning is a wonderful thing, tis a bit like Guy Fawkes Night, I suppose. The shortest day of the year, the longest night. We make ourselves a straw man. And as soon as the sun goes down, everyone in the village lights a flaming torch and we have ourselves a procession up to the headland. When we get to the stones, we light ourselves a big bonfire and have baked potatoes and the like. Tis a proper party. Some stay right through until the sun comes up, if it's not too perishing cold. It drives away the darkness, see? It makes the year turn so spring can come again. My Ted used to think it was magical when he was a child. But I don't suppose we shall be allowed that this year. Not with the war about to start and the blackout. They say not a chink of light should seep through our curtains. Ted has been busy all day fixing shutters to the windows. Twill be like living in a cave! Shame about the Burning. We could do with driving out the darkness this year more than ever. Maybe we'll do something else, eh? A party in the schoolroom for the children, perhaps. We'll need something to cheer us through the winter. I shall have a word with Lady Atherington. She likes to think she's in charge of village events."

To begin with, the lane ran along the valley more or less parallel with the river. It was hard to see the water, though. Hedges taller than fully grown men hemmed them in on either side. They were like the guards at Buckingham Palace, Alfie thought, pressed shoulder to shoulder, standing to attention. It made Alfie feel like the king, inspecting his troops.

Once in a while, they came to a gate and Alfie

glimpsed the countryside beyond, perfectly framed as if someone very clever had painted it.

When they reached a bend, the lane parted company with the river and started to head uphill. Alfie found it hard-going and was soon a little short of breath, but Auntie Bell talked without stopping.

"I do hope you'll like it on the farm with Ted and me, my birdie. I should hate for you to feel homesick. Now there's no electricity and no running water, so I dare say that might take some getting used to for a city boy like you. I made up a bed in the box room. Tis small, mind, but tis cosy and warm, right above the kitchen so it stays that way even when the weather turns cold. Got its own little staircase so it can be your private kingdom if you like. Used to be the maid's back in the day when we had servants but I thought it might be the nicest for a child. But if you don't like it, you can just say and we'll have a look see if there's a different room you'd prefer."

Alfie opened his mouth to say that the room sounded lovely, and he was sure he'd like it, but Auntie Bell's flow of words was unstoppable.

"Now, tis just Ted and I live on the farm," she went on. "Frankie comes up from the village to help with the milking every day, and any other odd jobs that Ted needs a hand with, sheep shearing and laying hedges and the like. We always need to bring in extra help come harvest, of course. Other than that, Ted and I get by on our own. There's plenty to do, mind. Maybe you'll be an extra pair of hands to help when you get the hang of things, eh? All our animals have got their own little ways and habits. We've got the cows, who are sweet souls. You can see them in that field over there, look. That one's Buttercup and Bluebell is next to her and there's Primrose and Pansy. I shall introduce you to them all tomorrow, so you can learn who's who. Our bull's called Widger and he's a handsome fellow – but don't go near him, no matter what. He lives in the stable next to the barn, so if you hear him moaning and groaning, just ignore it. He's an evil-tempered thing, impossible to handle. Tis only Ted who can manage him.

"We got a pig, too, of course. We don't ever name the pig. Best not to get attached, see? Poor thing will be for the chop soon. Tis always a hard day, pig killing. My Bill used to cry for a week beforehand! Didn't matter how often he told himself not to get fond of the creatures, he just couldn't help it. They're clever things, see? Cleverer than dogs even. Bill always said that God played a poor joke on pigs, making them so intelligent and so delicious. Bill hated killing time, but he always ate the pork. He loved a bit of crispy crackling, did Bill. And apple sauce of course."

The thought of roast pork and apple sauce seemed to divert her for a moment because she suddenly said, "The Bramleys will be ripe. I must get started on my chutneys!"

She looked at Alfie. "What was I saying before? Animals! That's right. I was telling you who's who. We got a fair few cats running about the place to keep the rats and mice down. Don't go trying to pet them, they'll scratch you as soon as look at you. And we got the dogs, Jake and Sam. They're working collies, mind, not pets. You mustn't go making a fuss of them, neither – Ted won't like it. He says it puts them off their work. We got the two carthorses. Ted uses them for the ploughing and suchlike. Makepeace and Blossom. Makepeace is inclined to nip if you're not careful. As for the other end! Don't ever go around the back of him – he'll take a sly kick if you give him the chance. And a little thing like you? He'd send you flying into next week. Blossom, though – she's soft as butter. You rub her between the ears, she'll love you for it. Blossom wouldn't hurt a fly. Maybe we can give you a ride on her, eh? You ever ridden a horse?"

Alfie shook his head. He wasn't sure whether or not he wanted to try it.

"Tell you what," said Auntie Bell. "When I take her

to be shod, I'll pop you up on her back, shall I? The world looks different from up there, my birdie. You feel like you can touch the clouds. You shall look like a prince sitting so high, the lord of all you survey."

Alfie liked the sound of that. He smiled shyly at Auntie Bell.

"Now, the geese – you have to watch them. They're better than the dogs for telling us when an intruder's about, but, if they think you're scared, they'll chase after you like demons. Tis in their nature. And if they pinch your skin in their bills, it doesn't half hurt. So if they come up behind you, turn and face them. Make yourself big. And if that doesn't work, grab the nearest one by the neck and give it a shake. They'll leave you alone then. Then there's the chickens... You can give me a helping hand with them if you like. They're all easy enough to deal with. All apart from Lady Atherington."

Auntie Bell darted Alfie a sideways look and laughed. "Yes, I named one after Her Ladyship. Tis a bit naughty of me, I suppose, but when you meet that bird, you'll understand why. They get shut up in the small barn at night to protect them from the foxes. Lady Atherington always lays her eggs up near the rafters where I can't hardly reach them, but maybe you'll find it easier, an agile lad like you. Don't you ever go mentioning I named a chicken after Her Ladyship, or I shall never hear the last of it. That's just between ourselves, a secret, like."

Her steady stream of chatter just kept on coming. Alfie was close to exhaustion. The light was fading but every time he thought they must be nearly there, they'd round another corner and another length of lane stretched ahead. Auntie Bell didn't seem to need to breathe like Alfie did, or notice the steepness of the hill. Alfie – who wasn't used to walking so far or so fast – found himself gasping.

"Oh, Alfie!" cried Auntie Bell when she noticed him struggling. "Why didn't you say you were tired? There's me rabbiting on nineteen to the dozen while you're getting worn out. Stop and sit down for a while. Look, see, you can perch on the gate there. Tis our land from here right to that hill yonder."

Alfie did as he was told, climbing the gate and sitting down to look at the view. The hill sank into a wooded valley. Beyond that rose another hill, criss-crossed with hedges, with not a house in sight, nor a single person other than him and Auntie Bell. He couldn't hear anything but the wind in the trees and the birds singing. No cars. No buses. No bustling shoppers. No bells ringing. No doors slamming.

He breathed in. That air! So clear and clean

without the smells of soot or traffic, women's perfume, men's sweat. Just this heady mix of vegetation and something vaguely salty that Alfie couldn't identify.

A picture of Alfie's fellow evacuees flashed into his mind. On the bus that brought them here, in between bouts of retching, Jack Davies had looked out of the window at the open countryside and wailed to his sister, "There's nothing here, Vi!"

And Violet had turned to Miss Bottomley and whispered in horror, "What are we going to do, Miss?"

Alfie's response was the opposite. His heart was beating faster, but not with fear. Somewhere inside him a wild excitement had taken root. All that space! Those fields, those woods, those valleys just waiting to be discovered... He felt like an explorer, about to set off on an expedition. And yet he also felt strangely comfortable and relaxed, as if he was returning home after a long time away. He felt ... *welcome*.

While Alfie was struggling to understand how it was possible to feel two different things at the same time, the slowly sinking sun came out from behind a cloud. At the far end of the wooded valley below him, a line of sparkling light appeared suddenly.

"What's that, Auntie Bell?" he asked, pointing.

"Oh, bless you, my birdie!" she said, smiling. "That's the sea."

COOMBE FARM

The farmhouse snuggled just below the brow of the hill facing towards the sea, stone and slate settled deep into the land as if it had grown there. It was almost dark by the time they reached it, but Alfie could see there was a yard behind the house with a large barn on the far side and two smaller buildings set against it.

"We'll go in through the kitchen door," Auntie Bell said, as she led Alfie across the cobbles. "We only use the front one if the vicar comes calling."

Next to an open-sided shed was a block of stables from which two huge horses' heads looked out. As Alfie and Auntie Bell approached, one of them tossed its mane, laid back its ears and bared yellowing teeth. The other whickered a soft, gentle greeting.

"Stop your nonsense, Makepeace," Auntie Bell told the first.

"Hello, Blossom!" she called to the second. "This here's Alfie. I shall introduce you properly tomorrow. But right now tis time to feed the poor lad."

She ushered Alfie into the farmhouse kitchen. Supper consisted of a cup of tea and a slice of freshly baked bread slathered with butter. A piece of ham that was as thick as Alfie's little finger was laid on top. Alfie chewed slowly and sleepily. Once he'd swallowed his last mouthful, Auntie Bell said, "Early night for you, young man. I shall show you around properly in the morning."

Picking up Alfie's suitcase, she climbed the back stairs to the box room. He followed close behind.

"Is it all right?" she asked, opening the door. "You must say if it's too small."

Alfie stepped into a room that was indeed tiny. But it was tiny in a nice way, Alfie thought, like a nest or a den. The ceiling sloped so steeply that it would have been hard for an adult to move anywhere without banging their head. A lighted candle threw flickering shadows across it. His own private kingdom was as warm and as welcoming as Auntie Bell.

"It's lovely," said Alfie.

A thick, brightly coloured patchwork eiderdown

lay on the bed. There was a chamber pot on the floorboards underneath, Auntie Bell told him. The toilet was just across the yard but it was best not to use it at night, she warned, because of the rats.

"The cats do their best to keep the numbers down, but we'll never be rid of them entirely, I'm afraid."

She'd filled a jug of water and put it on the washstand so he could wash his face and clean his teeth, but Alfie was too tired for that. As soon as Auntie Bell left him, he changed into his pyjamas, crawled under the eiderdown and fell asleep almost immediately. When Auntie Bell came up five minutes later to tuck him in, Alfie was completely dead to the world.

There was a noise. Faint, but persistent. And getting slowly but steadily louder.

Alfie was so deeply asleep that it took some time for the sounds to penetrate his brain. Waking was like swimming up from the bottom of a well: sluggish and arduous. When he surfaced, he felt dazed. For a few moments, he had no idea where he was. Or when. Was it day or night? It was so dark in the box room he couldn't see his hand in front of his face.

The strange, unfamiliar noise was coming from outside. Soothing, rhythmic thuds, getting closer with each heartbeat. The thudding was interspersed with the low, gentle rumbles of one creature calling to another. The sounds pulled Alfie out of his bed and over to the window.

Did he dare open the blackout shutters? Was he allowed? His hand paused on the latch for a moment before he realized that if it was pitch dark *in* the room it was impossible for him to let any light *out*.

When he tugged open Ted's carefully crafted shutters, he was blinded by the brightness of the sunshine. He blinked a few times before he could take in the scene below.

A river of huge animals was flowing along the lane towards the farm. What on earth were they?

Cows!

He'd seen black-and-white ones from the train yesterday. And then on the walk here Auntie Bell had pointed some out in a far field that were chestnut red just like the ones he could see streaming through the open gate and into the farmyard.

Alfie wondered if they'd escaped. Should he call Auntie Bell? But no... She was out there, behind the cows, walking alongside a tall young man who might be Ted and a second, shorter and much older man, who might be Frankie from the village. Two black-and-white dogs were nipping at the cows' heels, driving them along. The grown-ups followed the last of them into the yard and closed the gate, and slowly, calmly, the animals walked into the open-sided shed and lined up, one behind the other, like passengers at a bus stop.

Auntie Bell caught sight of Alfie at the window. Waving and smiling, she called up to him, "You're awake, my birdie! Come down and meet the girls!"

MUCK AND MAGIC

When they'd spotted the cows from the train yesterday, Billy Figgs had asked Miss Bottomley what they were.

"Cows," she'd replied.

"What are they for?" Billy had asked.

"They give us milk," she said.

Billy had snorted in disbelief. "You're joking, ain't you?"

The children had all looked agog at Miss Bottomley, awaiting her reply.

"You bunch of ignoramuses!" she said with an embarrassed laugh. "Where on earth do you imagine milk comes from?"

"From the shop, Miss," said Ned Smith.

"Out of a tin," added Stan Murphy helpfully.

"You sillies!" exclaimed Miss Bottomley. "It ends up in a tin on a shop shelf. It starts on a farm with a farmer taking it out of the cow."

The children looked at one another, baffled.

"How, Miss?" asked Jack Davies. "Where does he take it from?"

Miss Bottomley's description of the milking process had been vague. She'd gone red and used long, incomprehensible words the way grown-ups did if you asked where babies came from. At the end of her explanation, Alfie didn't really know any more than he had at the beginning. But Billy Figgs had somehow grasped the subject, for he announced loudly so the whole train could hear, "Milk comes out of a cow's bosoms!"

The children had erupted into storms of giggles and, no matter how often Miss Bottomley told them to stop being so silly, repeated outbursts of hysterical laughter had rippled through the carriage right until they'd reached the end of the line and had to get on the bus. It had been quite a relief for her when travel sickness wiped the smiles off their faces.

Alfie hadn't quite believed her outlandish story, but now was his chance to discover the truth. He pulled on the clothes he'd worn yesterday and hurried downstairs.

When he reached the door to the yard, Alfie paused, his hand resting on the latch. A wave of sudden shyness overwhelmed him. Auntie Bell had been so welcoming the day before, but how might Ted feel about having a strange boy from London staying at the farm? What would Frankie think of him? And the cows? Would they know that he'd never seen one up close before and that he was a bit scared of them?

There was only one way to find out.

"Bless you!" said Auntie Bell as Alfie stepped into the yard. "I was going to let you sleep on, this being your first day. I thought you'd need to rest after the journey, but it's good to see you up already. Going to come and give me a hand?"

Ted and Frankie were already busy milking. Ted had the same round face and apple-red cheeks as Auntie Bell, Alfie noticed. Frankie had a lean, leathery, weather-beaten look, as if he spent all his life out of doors. Both men cast a friendly nod in Alfie's direction as he started to pick his way across the yard towards Auntie Bell, trying to avoid the vast pancakes of muck. A sudden roar from a stable on the other side made Alfie freeze. A second angry bellow was followed by a loud thud as whatever it was hurled itself against the stable door. Through the open top half, Alfie got a glimpse of horns.

A memory flashed into Alfie's mind. Miss Bottomley reading her class a story at school. A Greek myth about a horned beast kept hidden in a labyrinth that ate human flesh. A Minotaur!

Should he run away?

"Don't look so scared, Alfie!" Auntie Bell called cheerfully. "'Tis just Widger, calling to his lady friends. He's our bull, remember? Told you he was an evil-tempered old thing."

Another thud. Another raging roar. Both of which the cows completely ignored.

Heart still racing, Alfie carried on across the yard to Auntie Bell.

"This here is Primrose," she said, leading Alfie into the milking shed, where the cows were standing side by side in stalls, tugging mouthfuls of hay from a manger that ran the length of the wall. "Primrose is the oldest of the ladies in the herd and the sweetest-natured of them all. Watch and learn, Alfie. Then maybe you can have a go."

Taking a three-legged stool, she sat herself down beside the cow and placed a bucket beneath Primrose. When Alfie bent down to see what was going on, he noticed a rounded, bulging sack of flesh under Primrose's belly with what looked like four sausages growing out at the bottom. Auntie Bell grasped two of them between her thumb and forefinger, then closed the rest of her fingers and squeezed. A jet of milk shot into the bucket.

"It's true!" Alfie gasped. "They keep milk in their bosoms!"

Auntie Bell chuckled, but not unkindly. "Udders," she said. "They're called udders. And these here are the teats. Want to have a try?"

Alfie took Auntie Bell's place on the stool. It was harder than it looked. He tried to copy what she had done but couldn't get a firm enough grip. Only when his fingers were aching with the effort and the placid Primrose was beginning to get irritated, did he manage to squeeze out a single jet of milk. It missed the bucket and squirted all over Auntie Bell's boot.

Alfie was horrified. He looked up, expecting her to be angry, but she was smiling at him.

"Nice try!" she said. "You shall get the hang of it in time, birdie. But for now you'd best let me take over."

Milking took a long, long time. When, at last, all the buckets had been strained and emptied into churns and the churns had been heaved into a stone water trough to cool, Auntie Bell said, "Ted and Frankie can drive the girls back to their field, Alfie. Let's you and I go and let the birds out, collect the eggs. Then we shall have breakfast. Nice bit of bacon do you? And after that, maybe you'd like to have an explore. Go off on your own for a bit? Get your bearings, like. How does that sound?"

It sounded to Alfie like the best thing in the entire world.

EXPLORING

"I saw you'd not brought much with you," Auntie Bell said after they'd finished their bacon and eggs. "I don't suppose your mother knew what she was sending you off to, did she? Not if she's lived in a city all her life. Poor woman! How a mother could bear to be parted from her child is beyond me. You must write to her this evening, tell her you got here safe. She'll be worrying herself sick, I shouldn't wonder. And your father too, no doubt?"

Alfie opened his mouth but no words came out. Auntie Bell took his silence for agreement.

"We must all make the best of it, I'm afraid," she said gently. "We shall have more hard times ahead, I don't doubt."

There was a pause and then Auntie Bell changed the subject.

"I looked out some old things of Ted's last night and got them cleaned up a bit after you'd gone to bed. I kept everything from when he was a boy, see? Never throw anything out, my Bill used to say. You never know when it might come in handy. And look how right he proved to be!" She looked at Alfie, suddenly anxious. "That's if you don't mind hand-me-downs?"

Alfie, who'd never worn anything but other people's cast-offs, shook his head.

Soon he was properly equipped for his expedition: laced into a pair of stout boots, with a woollen scarf wrapped twice around his neck, and buttoned tightly into a tweed coat so thick it could probably have stood up all by itself. He set off to explore with a rucksack on his back containing a sandwich, a jar of tea and two apples that Auntie Bell had plucked from a tree in the orchard at the side of the farmhouse.

"Don't want you succumbing to starvation," she said with a smile.

Somehow, she'd also found the time last night to draw him a map, which he studied carefully now. Squiggly lines for the rivers, dotted ones for the paths and wavy marks for the sea. It showed clearly that Coombe Farm was on a hill that sloped into two wooded river valleys on either side, with a field in front of the house that ran right up to the cliff edge.

The path across it divided into two. If you followed the left-hand fork, you could go along the cliffs, down through the woods and find a waterfall where a river tumbled into the sea. There was a bridge across it, and then a path up to a pointed bit of land that jutted out into the ocean like the prow of a ship. Auntie Bell had drawn a few tiny marks on it. Little oblongs arranged in a circle, like the marks on a clock face. Alfie had no idea what they were supposed to be and he was too shy to ask. In any case, he was more interested in the path that went to the right. That one zigzagged down through the woods to where the second river widened out and flowed across the beach into the waves.

"You could explore the cove a little, maybe, if it's low water," Auntie Bell said. "But you must watch out for when the tide turns. Do you know about tides, Alfie dear?"

Alfie told her that yes, he did. He'd lived by the Thames all his life so he knew about the water's ebb and flow and the irresistible strength of the currents.

"And, for heaven's sake, don't go climbing the cliffs, neither. They crumble sometimes and I should hate for you to have an accident."

"I won't," said Alfie, who, although he'd never had any idea of going rock climbing before, was now beginning to think it sounded like fun. "Promise."

Reassured, Auntie Bell informed Alfie that there were stepping stones across the river and, if he got himself to the other side, he could either go down onto the beach or he could walk upriver all the way to the village.

"Whatever takes your fancy. It's a muddy old path, mind. But now you've got a proper pair of boots on, you shall be fine. Come home by teatime. And don't go getting lost, or we shall have to send Jake and Sam to round you up."

Alfie set off. In one hand, he clutched the map. In the other, he carried a walking stick. The geese had tried to chase him when they'd been let out of the small barn that morning and no amount of making himself look big had helped. Auntie Bell had shooed them off, clapping her hands, flapping her arms, driving them away from Alfie but she had been worried about what might happen if she wasn't in the yard when he returned to the farm.

"Just swing that there stick at them. And yell for help if you need to. I shan't be far away."

He could worry about the geese later, Alfie thought. Meanwhile, he was planning to go to the beach. He'd only had a distant glimpse of the sea yesterday – a dazzling line of silver that had appeared when the sun came out. He couldn't even begin to imagine what it might look like up close and was desperate to find out.

It turned out that planning and actually doing something were two different things.

Alfie didn't make a conscious decision. He wasn't aware of changing his mind. Yet, when he reached the spot where the paths diverged, he found his feet carrying him off to the left. Towards the waterfall. The bridge. And the stones.

THE STANDING STONES

The day was sunny, and unusually warm for September. It wasn't long before the scarf was folded and tucked safely into the rucksack and Alfie was carrying the tweed coat over his shoulder.

He walked along the cliff path, marvelling at the vast expanse of azure-blue sea that stretched from the foot of the cliffs to the far horizon. He knew perfectly well that the Earth was round, but, looking at the line where sky met sea, it was easier to imagine the world was flat and that, if you sailed too far, you'd fall over the edge into nothingness.

Alfie's feet carried him down the path into a wooded valley. The trees reminded him of the ones he'd seen the day before through his magnifying glass. Similar, but different. Damp, dark leaves lay underfoot, but the ones overhead, though still mostly green, were beginning to be tinged with the yellow and red of autumn. He rubbed his hand over each trunk he passed, savouring the cool, grey smoothness of one, the mossy dampness of the next.

Yesterday he'd seen blue flowers carpeting the ground and breathed in their heady scent. There were none here, though. And the ferns that had been uncoiling like springs were fully out and turning brown with age. The birdsong – when it came – was sparse and muted, not the great chorus he'd heard the day before, yet the sense of wonder and the feeling of freedom were the same. Here he was, in what seemed like an earthly paradise.

He'd been so lucky! Luckier than any of the other evacuees, probably. He'd seen how tightly Violet Davies clutched her brother's hand when they were told to be seen and not heard. Billy Figgs had worn a look of pure panic when he'd been led away by the man who wanted help with the deliveries. Even Miss Bottomley had seemed scared by the prospect of staying at the Manor with Lady Atherington.

When Alfie reached the bottom of the valley, all thoughts of his fellow evacuees vanished from his mind. An odd sensation began to creep through Alfie's veins. It was faint to begin with. A vague stirring, deep in his belly, almost like the beginnings of a tummy ache. As it spread, it became an itching impatience that made him want to move faster.

He reached the wooden bridge that crossed the river and paused for a moment in the middle. The water flowed fast between slabs of rock, and there, just a few feet beyond, plunged over the edge of the land and into the sea.

It was a magnificent sight, but Alfie didn't pause to admire the waterfall for long. Something seemed to be tugging him towards the winding path that led up to the headland. Telling him, *Come here. Hurry up! Why are you taking so long?*

Alfie obeyed the strange calling, but the path was steep and Alfie, not used to such violent exercise, was soon out of breath. A stitch began to clutch at his side, so he stopped halfway up the slope until it eased. The woods were thicker here, the trees growing tightly together, branches interweaving, almost blotting out the sky. They were so different from the ones in the park in London, where his mother sometimes took him. Those were cut into shape every spring. Whole branches got lopped off at the top so they had a stunted, crippled look. And they were always covered in layers of city grime.

He leaned against a tree, feeling its rough, deeply

grooved bark pressing into his back. It was as if it had been raked all over with a giant fork. Looking up, he noticed its leaves were a different shape from the smooth-barked trees on the other side of the path. Dimly, Alfie began to perceive that maybe they were different kinds. He wondered if they had different names and whether he could learn them.

When the pain in his side had eased, Alfie carried on. The trees thinned gradually as he neared the top of the slope and then, at last, the landscape changed as he emerged from the wood. He had reached the headland, where an open stretch of grass and purple heather jutted out to sea.

And there at the furthest end, outlined against the sky, stood the stones. The sight of them knocked the breath out of Alfie's chest for a moment. When Auntie Bell had mentioned stones the day before, he had had no idea what she was talking about. If he'd been asked to picture them, he'd have imagined something the size of small cobblestones. The kind of thing girls threw into chalked squares when they were playing hopscotch, or Billy's lot threw at the ducks in the park.

These were taller than Ted. Slim. Bolt upright. Ten of them, standing in a perfect circle.

They were like soldiers, standing to attention,

thought Alfie. And then he contradicted himself. No ...
not soldiers. Soldiers were told what to do. They were
given orders and had to obey. These were more like
... what? Princes, maybe? Knights in armour? Heroes
from the Greek myths? There was something... Alfie
struggled to find the right word. Imposing. That was it.
There was something imposing about them.

Why were they grouped like that, in a perfect circle,
like people about to hold hands and start dancing?
No ... that was wrong too. They were serious, these
stones. Almost like they had a job to do. It was like
they were guarding something. Maybe there was
something precious buried in the middle of the circle:
a treasure chest, perhaps. Or, his mind still running
on the Greek myths, a golden fleece! He needed to get
a closer look.

Alfie approached the stones quietly and cautiously,
as if they were living beings that might suddenly turn
on him. He realized his heart was racing.

Stupid! he told himself. *They haven't got feelings.*
They're just stones. Rocks.

And yet somehow they were more than that. How
had they got there? Who had stood them up like that?
And why?

Alfie walked slowly and carefully around the edge
of the stone circle, almost on tiptoes. He could see

there was nothing in the middle – the idea of the stones standing guard over something was what his mother would call a "silly fancy". And, yet, he felt it would be wrong to set foot inside the circle. It would be ... what? Like going into somebody's house without asking. Or interrupting a private conversation. It would be intruding. And he didn't want to disturb the stones. It was as if they were waiting for something.

The words slipped into his head as if they had been whispered in his ear.

Not something.

Someone.

Alfie didn't get back to the farmhouse until the sun was sinking into the sea, turning it from azure blue to blood red. He'd spent the entire day on the headland, eating his picnic, drinking his jar of cold tea, sitting in the grass, his mind buzzing with questions about the stones. By the time he walked into the yard at Coombe Farm, the evening milking had been done and Frankie and Ted were herding the cows back to their field. Auntie Bell had shut in the geese and the chickens and was starting to think about preparing supper.

Alfie burst into the kitchen, questions tumbling out of his mouth, falling over one another in their eagerness to be heard.

Auntie Bell, who'd barely managed to get two words out of Alfie since his arrival, was astonished by his sudden chattiness.

"How old are the stones?" he asked. "How long have they been there? Why are they in a circle like that? What does it mean? How did they get up there? Did they sort of grow like trees? Can stones do that? Or did someone carry them up? Like a giant or something? What's the circle for?"

She smiled at him, but Auntie Bell – who Alfie had assumed could talk for England on any subject under the sun – had surprisingly little to say.

"Tis just where we go for the Burning, my birdie," she said with a shrug. There was a moment's pause and then, rubbing her hands together, she changed the subject. "Now ... what shall we have for our supper? I wonder. How would a nice bit of pie suit you?"

MR CHAMBERLAIN'S DECLARATION

Alfie's mother had always insisted that Sunday was a day of rest. If she was in a rare good mood and the weather was fine, they'd go to the park after church. If she had one of her headaches, Alfie would tiptoe around the house so as not to disturb her. He didn't always succeed. Sometimes she ordered him out and he'd spend the whole day wandering up and down the street trying to avoid Billy Figgs. Sundays in London always seemed to last for ever.

But Sundays at Coombe Farm were going to be different, Alfie realized. It was clear from the moment Auntie Bell called up the stairs, "Time to get up, Alfie dear. There's work to be done."

It seemed that cows didn't care what day of the week it was; they still needed to be milked. Eggs still needed to be collected, the sheep still needed to be checked, and the pig and the geese and the horses and dogs still needed to be fed.

On his second morning at Coombe Farm, Alfie went along with the grown-ups at first light to bring in the cows. Auntie Bell had told him not to make a fuss of the dogs. The trouble was, no one had told the dogs not to make a fuss of *him*. The moment he stepped into the yard, they greeted Alfie as if he was a long-lost friend. Jake planted his two front paws on Alfie's chest and gave his face a good lick. Sam circled him, tail wagging furiously. When they set off for the field, the dogs trotted along beside Alfie, mouths open in idiotically happy grins, until Ted's whistle brought them to heel.

Alfie thought Ted might be cross but the farmer seemed more amused than angry, giving Alfie a nod and a brief smile the same as he had the day before. Ted might have the face and apple-red cheeks of his mother, but in every other way he couldn't be more different. A strong, silent slab of a man, Ted was; as quiet as Auntie Bell was talkative. Yesterday morning, he'd said only "How do?" to Alfie. Today he didn't even say that much. Two words. That was the sum total of their conversation so far. Yet, strangely, it was enough. The farmer treated Alfie as if he was a table or a chair – something that just belonged at Coombe Farm. Alfie, who was in awe of the man who could handle the fearsome Widger, was grateful for Ted's silent acceptance. He wouldn't really have known what to say to Ted anyway.

Once all the morning work was done, Auntie Bell cooked breakfast. After that, it was time to get changed into their Sunday best and go to church.

They drove to the village on a horse-drawn cart. Bad-tempered Makepeace laid his ears back when he saw Alfie and stamped irritably when the boy climbed up next to Ted. Auntie Bell followed and the three of them sat wedged tightly together as Ted flicked the reins and the horse moved off with a sullen grunt. Ted was looking desperately uncomfortable in a starched shirt and smart jacket. Auntie Bell had a hat perched perilously on her head. Alfie was wearing an itchy woollen pullover of Ted's and long trousers.

"Reverend Braithwaite's dry as dust, I'm afraid,"

Auntie Bell told Alfie. "And he uses such long words! I can't follow most of what he says in his sermons. If your mind wanders, Alfie, I shan't go blaming you. Lord knows, mine always does! And I dare say he'll have a lot to talk about this morning."

Alfie wasn't really listening to her. The seat on the cart was so high up he could see over the hedges. As they left the farmyard, he looked over towards the stones. He could see the headland in the distance and just about make out the circle. It was strange because when he'd been up there yesterday, he'd looked across to the farm but hadn't been able to see it. In fact, he hadn't been able to see the road at all, or the hedges either side of it. *That's a bit odd, isn't it?* Alfie thought. And then he told himself not to be so silly. Farms and roads couldn't disappear! He couldn't have been looking in the right place.

The village church was a lot smaller than the one Alfie had gone to in London. The walls were made of big, uneven, oddly shaped grey stones, not neat, rectangular red bricks. Lady Atherington's dogs were tied up at the gate and the parishioners had to edge carefully past them. As he walked up the path, Alfie noticed that some of the headstones in the graveyard had been there so long that the names of the people lying beneath had completely worn away.

Inside, the atmosphere seemed tense and strained. Children that Alfie assumed must be locals were eyeing the evacuees as if they were creatures from another planet. Some looked simply curious. Others seemed openly hostile. The woman who Auntie Bell had said was best avoided – Mrs Copper – was sitting with a severe-looking old man and a boy about Alfie's age. The boy was glaring at Billy Figgs, who was sitting across the aisle from him, eyes fixed forward pretending he hadn't noticed. Sitting in a pew with Ted on one side and Auntie Bell on the other, Alfie felt perfectly safe but he noticed that the twins, Carrie and Claire, were holding each other's hands so tightly their knuckles were white. Violet and Jack Davies were both looking pale and Jack's eyes were red-rimmed as if he'd been crying.

Auntie Bell was right about the vicar. He was old, slightly bent-backed with paper-thin skin that wrinkled into folds like a napkin. He mumbled a few words of welcome to the evacuees and the service began. When he started his sermon, he didn't look at his congregation, but kept his eyes on the wad of paper he'd laid on the lectern, reading out what was written there in a whispery monotone. He was talking about testing times and how the strongest metal is forged in the hottest fire and the necessity for obeying the will of God and doing one's duty to king and country. Alfie made a valiant effort to follow but the vicar's sentences kept turning corners and, before long, Alfie had lost all sense of what he was saying. Beside him, Auntie Bell was already stifling a yawn. Alfie sank lower and lower down in the pew. His mind drifted off to what he could do after lunch. If he was allowed out again, he'd go to the beach, he thought. He'd resist the tug of the stones this time. He really had to get a closer look at the sea.

As the vicar's voice droned on and on, Alfie's eyelids grew heavier and heavier and he started to doze.

The sudden pressure of Auntie Bell's hand on his jerked Alfie awake. He was dimly aware that time had passed. Five minutes? An hour? Alfie couldn't tell. Something in the church had changed. For a moment, Alfie thought that Auntie Bell had noticed he'd fallen asleep and was angry with him. When he glanced up at her, he saw she was looking at Ted, her apple-red cheeks now drained of colour. Her jaw was set as if she was struggling not to cry and she was squeezing Alfie's hand so tight he thought she might crush his fingers. Ted was hanging his head but his back was rigid.

The vicar wasn't speaking any more. Someone else was. It was a voice Alfie vaguely recognized, one he'd heard when Mum listened to the news on the wireless. Was that the prime minister? Yes... Mr Chamberlain's voice was coming through a wireless. How had a wireless set got into the church?

It sounded like he was saying a prayer. But it also sounded like he was making a speech. The tone was serious. Solemn. It took Alfie a moment or two to make sense of the words.

"Now may God bless you all and may He defend the right. For it is evil things that we shall be fighting against – brute force, bad faith, injustice, oppression and persecution – and against them, I am certain that the right will prevail."

That seemed to be the end of it. There was a horrible, tense silence and Alfie realized he'd missed something terribly important. It seemed as if the whole congregation was braced and holding its breath. And then everyone exhaled in a collective, sorrowful sigh. Before anyone could turn to speak to one another, the vicar was on his feet again, leading them in more prayers for strength and fortitude and other things that Alfie didn't understand.

At last, it was over. They were spilling out of the church, and into the graveyard. It was only when

Auntie Bell stopped to talk to Lady Atherington that Alfie realized what everyone had been dreading for ages had finally happened. He'd slept through the prime minister's declaration, but England was now at war with Germany.

THE DARKNESS

The threat of war had been looming like a dark cloud on the horizon for so long that Alfie had almost grown used to it. He couldn't remember a time when grown-ups didn't gather on street corners or stand in shop queues arguing about Herr Hitler and Mr Chamberlain and what was happening in Germany. At school, they had been practising their gas-mask drill every day for months. The grass in the park had been dug up to make way for an air-raid shelter. Children like Alfie had been evacuated from the cities. Yet the preparations had all been "just in case". Grown-ups had hoped and prayed and wished right up until the very last minute that a miracle would occur. It hadn't. And now what had only been pretend was real. Men would fight. Bombs would fall. People would die. And others would get damaged in mind and body, like old Mr Moore. How would he cope with the news? Alfie wondered. Would they put him away, like they kept threatening to? Alfie couldn't bear the thought.

By the end of the service, the atmosphere inside the church had been brittle enough to break. As the congregation emerged into the bright sunshine, the grown-ups visibly braced their shoulders and pasted smiles onto their faces. They were going to be brave for the sake of the children. Already they were talking in voices that were slightly too cheerful, making weak jokes and laughing at them slightly too loudly.

Lady Atheringon and Auntie Bell had exchanged a few comments about the war, then Lady Atherington suddenly asked, "How's the boy settling in?" She looked at Alfie so sharply he took a step back, as if he'd been pecked. "All well and good?"

"All very well, thank you, Your Ladyship," replied Auntie Bell smoothly.

"And you?" Her Ladyship said, prodding Alfie in the chest. "Not giving Mrs Hartland any trouble, I hope?"

"None at all," Auntie Bell answered for him. "Alfie's being a big help. Getting the hang of things very nicely, he is. We shall make a farmer of him yet, you mark my words."

Perhaps in order to deflect any more questions,

Auntie Bell said, "I was wondering, Your Ladyship...
Maybe we should put our thinking caps on. We
shan't be able to have the Midwinter Burning this
year, shall we? Not with a war on and the blackout
and such. Perhaps we should do something else. For
the children, like. Cheer us all up when tis dark and
gloomy. A nice party, maybe?"

"If we are to do anything at all," the vicar said,
overhearing her and coming over, "let us make it
something appropriate to the Christian calendar.
We're not heathens, after all. I suggest a nativity play."

A shout cut through all the chatter in the graveyard.
"The Burning! We got to have the Burning!"

Everyone fell silent and turned to look at the man
who'd shouted.

He was old. Frail-looking. But his eyes were blazing
with rage. His hand was resting on the shoulder of the
boy who'd been glaring at Billy Figgs in church. The
old man was using him like a walking stick. Sour-
faced Mrs Copper was a step or two behind.

"Morning," said Auntie Bell brightly. Her mouth
was smiling but her eyes told a different story. "Mr
Copper. Mrs Copper." And then to the boy, "Morning,
Joe." Looking back at the old man, she asked, "How's
your lumbago this morning?"

Mr Copper completely ignored her. "We got to

have the Burning!" he told the vicar. "The Burning's old. Older than the church, older than Jesus, even. We got to find some way of doing it, war or no war. Else the Darkness shall come, and then where will we be?"

Alfie felt a prickle of alarm. Something felt odd. When Auntie Bell had first told him about the Midwinter Burning, she'd talked about dark nights, the year turning, and spring coming back. It had sounded normal. Natural. But when Mr Copper mentioned the Darkness it sounded sinister, as if the word had a capital D. Like the Darkness was a thing. A power, maybe. Or a creature, with a will of its own.

The words were out of Alfie's mouth before he knew he wanted to ask the question.

"What's the Darkness?"

Mr Copper blinked at the interruption, and his blazing eyes found Alfie. He grinned but there was nothing friendly in that look. It was more like one of Lady Atherington's dogs baring its teeth.

"You don't want to know that," Mr Copper said softly. "Lonely little lad like you. Best hope you never find out."

LOW TIDE

Declaring loudly that there were things to be done at the farm, Auntie Bell hurried Alfie away from the church and back to the cart. As Ted drove them out of the village, she told Alfie to pay absolutely no attention to anything Mr Copper ever said, "Not now nor in the future. He's a daft old thing. Not right in the head. Hasn't been for years, poor man. Doesn't mean no harm, not really, but he will get these ideas."

Before Alfie could ask, "What ideas?", she changed the subject.

"What will you do this afternoon, my birdie? Explore the beach, maybe? Tis a lovely day for it."

The prospect of the sea put all other thoughts out of Alfie's head. He'd marvelled at it from the clifftops yesterday and was desperate for a really close look at that vast expanse of water. Maybe he could even have a paddle in it?

Once he'd changed out of his Sunday best, Alfie, instead of eating lunch at the farmhouse with Auntie Bell and Ted, set off with a picnic all of his own packed into the rucksack.

He felt the same tug, just under his ribs, when he reached the spot where the paths divided, pulling him towards the stones. This time he steadfastly ignored it, turning slowly and deliberately away from the headland. Instead, he went to the right and zigzagged down through the woods until he reached the river and the stepping stones and the beach.

The sea was nothing short of a miracle, Alfie thought as he sat in the sunshine with his picnic, gazing at the endlessly changing water. The waves were mesmerizing, an indigo blue that paled to luminous turquoise when they reared their heads and the sunlight shone through, foaming into white as they broke on the shore and were then dragged back to the sea. The sight, the sound, the smell – he could have watched for ever. Yet there were also rock pools to explore with tiny fish that darted from shadow to shadow. Crabs, scuttling sideways. Red things that looked like flowers but whose fronds stuck to Alfie's finger when he brushed against them, clinging on to him as if with tiny hands. And, at the foot of the cliffs, there were dark, damp caves that might house a dragon or a sea monster.

Alfie wandered the length of the cove and back again, keeping an eye on the tide as Auntie Bell had warned him. The previous high tide had deposited all sorts of items. Driftwood. Bits of fishing net. The odd jam jar and even a whole tin of condensed milk.

When he returned to the farm at tea time, blissfully content, he was yawning from having inhaled so much rich sea air.

"It has that effect if you're not used to it," Auntie Bell told him. "Early to bed for you again, Alfie dear."

On his first two nights at Coombe Farm, Alfie had fallen asleep almost instantly. That Sunday night, despite the yawning earlier, he lay in bed watching the strange shadows thrown across the ceiling in the flickering candlelight.

Auntie Bell came to tuck him in, pulling the sheets and blankets so tight he felt swaddled, like the baby Jesus. As she kissed him on the forehead, there was a screech and a hoot from outside that made Alfie jump.

"Nothing to worry about," she said soothingly. "'Tis only an owl, calling to its friends. They have right regular conversations the whole night long sometimes. There are all kinds of things out there that you might hear. Badgers, foxes... Just animals, going about their business. Nothing to be afraid of. Different from what you've grown up with, I expect? But you'll get used to it, Alfie dear. Sometimes, when the wind's in the right direction, you can hear the sea from up here. I always find that soothing. Like a lullaby. Mother Nature, rocking you to sleep. Unless it's blowing a gale, of course!" She smiled. "That's Mother Nature in a temper. Nothing very soothing about that!"

She said goodnight once more and blew out the candle. Alfie lay in the dark listening to the night sounds beyond the window. The hoot came again. Then something barked. One of the dogs, maybe? A fox? A badger? What noise did badgers make? What did they even look like? Something small cried out – a mouse?

They were just animal sounds, Alfie told himself. Normal and natural, even if they were new to him.

That soft hissing he could hear? That must be the sea. It was soothing, he told himself. A lullaby. Just the rolling waves, that was all. It couldn't possibly be what it sounded like. There couldn't possibly be people out there. Whispering.

FARM LIFE

Alfie had a whole week on the farm before starting at the village school. Life fell into a quietly comfortable routine. At sunrise every morning, he went with Ted, Auntie Bell and Frankie to help bring in the cows for milking. Being out at that time was a bit like watching the tide turn, Alfie thought, with one world gently giving way to another. The day animals were just beginning to stir and the night animals were heading off to sleep. He'd catch glimpses of them sometimes. On Monday, something white fluttered across the yard that Alfie thought was a paper bag until Auntie Bell told him it was a barn owl. The next day, he caught an orange-gold flash that turned out to be a fox sloping away to its den. It had looked at Alfie with wild, amber eyes before disappearing through a hole in the hedge.

The following morning, he saw a roly-poly black-and-white creature trundling towards the woods that he later learned was a badger.

Once the milking was done, Ted would go off, sometimes with Frankie but more often on his own, to do whatever needed doing – mending fences, laying hedges, repairing gates, trimming sheep's hooves. The list of Ted's jobs seemed endless. As for Auntie Bell – there was cream to be separated and set to clot in the oven or churned into butter. There was cheese to be made and bread to be baked. Alfie helped with anything she asked, enjoying the warmth of the kitchen and the cool of the dairy and her constant chatter.

His own particular task was to let the poultry out of the small barn in the mornings and give them their breakfast. He soon found that he was engaged in a daily running battle with the geese. The moment he started to unbolt the door, they began hissing and honking. When he opened it, they came dashing out to attack him, necks outstretched, wings flapping, feathers flying. The ungrateful creatures treated Alfie as if he was a deadly enemy not their liberator. They flocked around him, snapping at his legs and arms with their bills, trying to nip his flesh, while Alfie wielded the walking stick like a sword, swishing it back and forth with one hand. With the other, he reached into the pouch of grain that was tied at his waist and threw handfuls of corn at them until the geese decided that food was more interesting than fighting.

Once the geese had settled down, all but one of the chickens would emerge from the small barn to help peck up the scattered grain. Alfie's next task was to collect their eggs, which would have been as easy as pie if the one remaining hen hadn't been Lady Atherington.

The other hens – five small brown ones that he couldn't tell apart, a white one with a gammy leg and a large black one – always laid their eggs in the cosy nest boxes that were stuffed with clean straw. They never even noticed when Alfie gathered them up. Lady Atherington, however, spurned cosiness and comfort. She roosted way up in the rafters and wouldn't budge when Alfie came into the barn. Every morning, she stayed exactly where she was, looking haughtily down her beak at Alfie, speckled feathers fluffed up with indignation that anyone would dare approach her. Alfie developed a technique of dislodging the hen with his walking stick before climbing the ladder to retrieve her egg but she always managed to land a scratch or a peck on him before the task was completed. On the fifth morning, she managed both, and he nearly dropped the egg as he tried to avoid her sharp beak.

Alfie was standing outside the barn with a basket of eggs, examining the long scratch on his right arm and the dotted peck marks on his left leg, when Auntie Bell called across the yard, "I'm off to get Blossom shod this morning, Alfie. Want to come along with me?"

Alfie smiled shyly at her.

"Yes, please!"

GHOST ROAD

Alfie had seen carthorses in London, pulling brewery drays along the streets, huge great creatures, with plaited manes and tails. They were so big he'd always felt a bit afraid of them and Makepeace's grumpiness had done nothing to persuade Alfie that horses might be friends. Auntie Bell had said she'd let him ride Blossom on the way to the blacksmith's. She'd promised that up there on the horse's back he'd feel like he could touch the clouds. The idea was too glorious to resist.

As Auntie Bell led Blossom out of the stable, she called Alfie over.

Up close, Blossom filled his whole field of vision, blotting out the sky, the farm, the fields beyond: he could see nothing but horse. She was gigantic.

Monstrous! Alfie was about to say that he'd changed his mind and, please, could he stay at the farm? Then, slowly and gently, Blossom lowered her great head and pressed it against Alfie's chest. The top of it fitted under his chin; her ears tickled either side of his face. Her nose brushed below his knees and she blew a puff of hot breath down onto his ankles. It felt strangely reassuring.

"What does she want?" Alfie asked nervously.

"Rub her between the ears, just there. That's right, birdie. Told you she was soft as butter, didn't I? You've got a friend for life now. Come on, let's get you up there."

Blossom's back seemed as broad and flat as the kitchen table. Alfie had to climb onto the gate in order to get up there and, even then, it was an undignified scramble. Not that Blossom seemed to mind. She stood perfectly still while Alfie tried sitting astride the way Auntie Bell had told him to but it was desperately uncomfortable. His legs stuck out at such extreme angles that Auntie Bell started to giggle.

"Oh, my dear!" she said. "I'm sorry. I know tisn't funny but you do look a picture!"

Alfie, who so hated being jeered at by Billy and his friends, found he didn't mind at all when it was Auntie Bell doing the laughing. There was no malice in it, and she had such a round, jolly face. He smiled and even found himself joining in.

"You can't go riding her like that," continued Auntie Bell, wiping tears of laughter from her cheeks. "You'll do yourself a mischief. How about you swing your left leg over her neck, eh? You best sit sideways, I think."

Once the manoeuvre was successfully executed, they set off, Auntie Bell leading the mild-mannered Blossom along while Alfie sat on top, clutching a bit of Blossom's mane in his right hand just in case he lost his balance. The horse's motion was no stranger than being on a tram or a bus and Alfie soon got the hang of it.

Auntie Bell had been right when she'd said the world looked different from the back of a horse. He'd been high up on the cart on Sunday, but then he'd been wedged between Auntie Bell and Ted. Now he was alone, he really did feel like the lord of all he surveyed.

They began their journey, making slow and stately progress along the lane that wound in lazy curves down the hill. As they rounded the first bend, Alfie looked over a gate and across the grassy fields to the wooded valley and the headland jutting out to sea.

The grass was lush and thick but he noticed a line of sparse growth cutting right across the middle of the fields, almost as if it had been mown. It was like the ghost of a road, heading directly to the stones. He twisted around, straining to look over his shoulder to see if it continued on the other side of the lane. And yes! Over the hedge the same straight line of sparse, short grass led down to the wooded valley. He could just about make out the chimneys of a huge house beyond the trees that had to be Atherington Manor.

Noticing Alfie squirming around, Auntie Bell asked, "Are you all right up there, birdie?"

"Yes," Alfie answered. "It just looked like there was a path or a road or something going across."

Auntie Bell smiled up at him. "Clever lad! Very well spotted. That's the old way to the stones, the one we used to take when His Lordship was alive. There was a gate there once, right opposite this one," she said, pointing to what was now a solid hedge. "But Her Ladyship put a stop to all that years ago."

"Then why can we still see it?"

Auntie Bell considered. "I don't rightly know... I suppose all those feet, tramping up and down for all those years, leaves its mark. Maybe it presses the soil so hard the grass can't grow tall there."

Alfie looked back at the headland. He could just make out the stones. Standing. Waiting. Calling.

It was as though an invisible length of string was

tied to his ribs and connected him to them. He felt it tighten and didn't like it. So he turned his face inland, towards the village, to see if he could spot the church spire poking up above the trees.

There were plenty of people out and about that Wednesday morning and Auntie Bell chatted to everyone she passed.

"How do, Joe? How do, Mr Copper?" she said when she saw the boy and his grandfather coming out of the village shop. "That grandson of yours grows bigger every day."

"Eating us out of house and home," Mr Copper replied sourly. He was talking to Auntie Bell, yet his eyes rested on Alfie. Alfie turned his head away but he could still feel that look of Mr Copper's burning into his skin. And he thought he heard the old man mutter to his grandson, "Little lad, just like that one there. One who didn't belong. That's how it started, I tell you."

Alfie didn't hear Joe answer, so he glanced at the boy to see how he'd reacted to his grandfather's words. Joe was looking up at Alfie with a smile on his face, but there was no warmth in it. None at all.

They moved on. When they reached the square, Alfie saw Violet with her brother Jack sitting on the doorstep of a neat, prim cottage like a pair of abandoned parcels. When Violet noticed Alfie, perched on top of the enormous horse, she stared at him with eyes as round as saucers. Jack's mouth dropped open and he pointed wordlessly at Blossom and turned to his sister, who said, "Hello, Alfie," as he rode past.

Alfie was so surprised he almost lost his balance. Violet never spoke to him. She was in Billy's gang and had always just stood there, watching Billy being horrible to him. Yet, today, she sounded shy. Friendly, almost. Alfie didn't know what to make of it and so he and Blossom went by without him saying anything.

They reached the smithy and it was time to dismount, which looked like it would be as tricky a manoeuvre as getting up had been.

"Right, birdie. How are we going to manage this? I wonder," said Auntie Bell to Alfie.

The ground suddenly seemed an awfully long way away. Alfie gulped.

"Tell you what... How about you turn over onto your tummy. Slide down her side and I shall catch you."

Alfie did as he was told, dropping with such speed that he almost knocked Auntie Bell clean off her feet. As they righted themselves, Alfie darted a glance in Violet's direction. He expected to see her laughing at him, but she gave him a shy, sympathetic smile.

"Friend of yours?" said Auntie Bell. "You can go play with her for a while if you like."

But Violet was too confusing.

"No, thank you," Alfie replied. "I'd like to see Blossom get her new shoes."

"Then that's what we'll do." Auntie Bell smiled. "Come on, my birdie."

BLACKBERRYING

"I have a fancy for an apple and blackberry pie," said Auntie Bell the following afternoon. "How about you go gather some berries for me, eh? The cows' field ... up there in the top right-hand corner. The blackberries always ripen first there. Take as long as you like, Alfie dear. Just be home by teatime, same as usual."

The notion of food growing in the hedgerows, free to anyone who cared to pick it, was another revelation to Alfie. Only a few days ago, his world had consisted of his street, the shop on the corner and his school a hundred yards away. Now it had expanded into something magical that teemed with extraordinary possibilities. Revelations had come in dizzying succession. Billy Figgs had been disgusted by the idea of where milk came from, remembered Alfie. How shocked was he going to be when he discovered that apples grew on trees, wool grew on sheep's backs and eggs came out of hens' bottoms? The thought of Billy's appalled face made Alfie suddenly laugh out loud. If Auntie Bell had told Alfie she could spin cow muck into gold, he'd have believed her.

So when he saw people moving through the woods as silently as ghosts, he didn't think twice about their strangeness.

He'd filled his bowl full of blackberries by then. The fattest and the juiciest had always seemed to be just a little bit further on and he'd moved along the hedge little by little until he'd come to a gate and a second field that sloped down to the wooded valley. He'd scrambled over it and picked along the length of the second hedge until he'd reached the gate that led into the woods.

The bowl was brimming with fruit. He could pick it up on the way back, he thought. Setting it down on the ground, he shinned up and over the gate.

He wandered happily but aimlessly through the woods until he came to a tree that bent over at the waist, curving almost to the ground as if it was reaching down to greet him. Years of being blown by salt winds had caused its branches to interlace and fuse together. Alfie had never climbed a tree before and wouldn't really know how to start. Yet this one looked as if it would be as easy as shinning up a ladder. It was positively inviting him to try.

And so Alfie climbed, slowly to begin with but then with more confidence. The branches thinned as he went up until eventually he got to a point where he wasn't sure they would bear his weight if he climbed any higher. Instead, he draped himself along a branch like a cat. The slanting sunlight turned the woodland into a golden-hued paradise and Alfie felt completely at peace. He shut his eyes and turned his face to the sky.

He felt the change before he saw it. Something had shifted, like a cloud passing in front of the sun. When he opened his eyes, the soft golden, autumnal light in the valley had disappeared. The vegetation looked thicker, wilder. The ground between the trees was hazed with the same blue flowers he'd seen when he'd been standing in the schoolroom waiting for Auntie Bell to come. The air was still, expectant, as if the whole wood was holding its breath.

He caught a movement out of the corner of his eye. Smelled that animal scent he'd smelled before. Something big was coming.

And then he glimpsed the creature below, picking its way through the undergrowth towards Alfie's tree. Not a cow, not a horse, not any kind of farm animal. It had spindle-thin legs and what looked like branches growing out of the top of its head. Sniffing the air, it paused for a moment, before moving on.

Alfie watched, mesmerized, until it was out of sight. And then he saw people, moving through the trees, hunched low to the ground, silent as shadows. It was hard to tell if they were men or women. A mix of both, Alfie thought, but they all had the same long black, wildly curling hair hanging loose about their shoulders, and wore the same strange clothes. Not ironed shirts and carefully knotted ties, not smart jackets and neatly pressed trousers, but weird leggings with a baggy sort of tunic on top. As they edged closer, Alfie noticed the poles in their hands – long sticks with pointed heads at one end. Were those spears? They reminded Alfie of a cowboys and Indians film he'd once seen in the cinema, when his mother had been in a rare good mood and had decided to treat him. Was this a game? Were they following the creature he'd seen? Could they be hunting it?

Whether it was terror or excitement, Alfie couldn't say. Something made him freeze to the branch. His heart thumped against his chest so hard he thought it might make the whole tree shake and give away his position. And if it did? There was a fierce intensity about these people. Alfie didn't want to be seen, especially by the one in front who was edging, inch by inch, closer to Alfie's tree. There was something peculiarly menacing about that one.

His stance reminded Alfie of Billy Figgs' father. Billy's dad was always ready for a fight. He'd use his fists to avenge any offence, real or imagined. Alfie had found himself on the wrong side of him once or twice simply for failing to get out of his sight fast enough. He didn't want to be noticed by this man, either. Alfie didn't dare breathe.

Wordlessly, with just a flick of his finger, the man directed the others. Two to the right, two to the left. Those three uphill, that one to follow him down the valley. And then he pointed to a boy of about Alfie's age, who looked different from the others. His hair was a fiery, coppery red, and tightly tangled as if it had never been brushed.

The boy was beckoned forward until he was standing in front of the man in charge. Alfie could see his face lighting up with eager excitement. There was a pause for one, maybe two heartbeats.

Then the man flapped his hand as if shooing the boy away.

The gesture was so familiar to Alfie he felt a painful stab of sympathy. The man didn't need to open his mouth. That flapping of the hand was as plain as day:

Go away. Get lost. You're not wanted here.

The man turned, and the hunters moved on silently, leaving the boy standing alone beneath Alfie's tree, watching until they were out of sight.

"A lonely little lad."

The words echoed in Alfie's head as the boy below let out a forlorn sigh, turned and walked away.

THE MR MOORE LOOK

"I saw some people," Alfie told Auntie Bell as he set the bowl of blackberries down on the kitchen table.

Auntie Bell stopped what she was doing and looked puzzled. "Where? In the field?"

"No, the woods. They were hunting, I think."

"Hunting?" Auntie Bell said. "All the way out here? Surely not! I didn't hear the pack. Were there dogs? People on horses?"

"No," said Alfie. "They were on foot. They had spears."

"Spears?" Auntie Bell echoed.

"Yes. And they were wearing funny clothes."

The lines on Auntie Bell's forehead grew deeper. The expression on her face was familiar, but Alfie couldn't quite read it for a moment. Then he realized she was looking at him the way people looked at old Mr Moore: as if he wasn't right in the head.

"Game, was it?" she said, her eyes fixed on him a little too intently. "Bit of make-believe? Something you were playing?"

And Alfie felt suddenly afraid and unsure. He didn't like Auntie Bell looking at him like that. He could feel her willing him to say that yes, he'd been playing. When he nodded, relief washed over her face and everything seemed all right again.

"What a powerful thing it is, to have an imagination!" she said, smiling and ruffling his hair. "You had me going there, for a minute. Mind you, Ted was just the same when he was your age. Used to fancy there were all kinds of creatures living in the woods. Ogres and imps and the like. Goblins. Trolls. My Bill would fill Ted's head so full of fairy tales the poor lad didn't know what was real and what wasn't half the time. Ted would spend hours looking for elves and pixies. You wouldn't think so now, would you, to look at him? Now it's just when to send the lambs to market, worrying about milk yields and whether the pig is fat enough for killing yet."

Alfie's mind was unsettled. *Was* he strange? he wondered. Not right in the head, like old Mr Moore?

He thought of his magnifying glass and of the two

young soldiers he'd seen laughing and chatting to the old man in the street. That hadn't been the first time. He recalled all the occasions he'd made the world blur and fade. Sometimes that was all it did. And sometimes fuzzy scenes would play out as if he was watching a slightly out-of-focus film. Ladies in big, hooped skirts, bonnets on their heads, climbing into horse-drawn carriages. The River Thames, crammed with ships making their way upriver to the docks. Ships, not forged from iron and powered by engines, but built from wood and driven by wind and sail. He'd never told anyone about what he sometimes saw because, well, who was there to tell? And, until this particular moment, he hadn't given it much thought. He'd sort of assumed that everyone did the same. But maybe they didn't. Maybe it was just him. And Mr Moore.

The people in the woods had been different, though, Alfie thought. They had been solid, not transparent. He'd seen and heard and smelled them. They were real. And yet the spears, their hair, their clothes ... they were so unlike anyone in the village. Unlike anyone he'd ever seen. There was something odd about the whole thing.

He felt slightly queasy, as if he'd eaten too much.

His mother said Mr Moore should be locked up. Put away. Suppose Auntie Bell thought the same about people who weren't right in the head? Suppose she sent him back to London? The thought brought Alfie close to tears.

He'd written a long letter to his mother on his second evening at Coombe Farm when Auntie Bell had told him to, telling her he'd arrived safely and was being well looked after. He'd described the cows and the horses and the dogs and everything else he could think of, filling two whole sides of paper.

The shortest of notes had come back from his mother a few days later, informing Alfie that she was frightfully busy, absolutely rushed off her feet with war work and wouldn't have time to write to him again. He'd felt relieved, rather than upset. He didn't need to feel guilty about not missing her because she so clearly wasn't missing him.

Suppose Auntie Bell sent him back? Back to his mother's headaches and her bad moods and her constant frown of irritation every time she looked at him... He wouldn't be able to stand it!

He had to keep quiet about the hunting party and the boy, that much was certain. He wouldn't breathe another word about them to Auntie Bell. But now – possibly for the first time in his life – he heartily wished he had a friend that he could talk to.

REFLECTIONS

Alfie didn't sleep well that night and the next day he was a little out of sorts. Unsettled by what he'd seen in the woods the day before, he was also worried about having lied to Auntie Bell. He'd told her that those people had been make-believe. It was bad to tell fibs, his mother always said. As bad as stealing. People got into trouble for that.

Maybe he *wasn't* lying? Suppose he'd somehow conjured them into being out of his imagination? Was such a thing possible?

He didn't know. And there was no one to ask. If Auntie Bell thought he was seeing things, he wouldn't be Alfie Right any more. He'd be Alfie Wrong and he couldn't bear the idea of that.

Auntie Bell, thinking that perhaps Alfie was lonely

or homesick, kept him by her side that morning. Her stream of chatter and good humour began to cheer him up after a while, but it was the pig who finally brought a smile to his face.

Auntie Bell was leaning over the door of the sty, emptying a bucket of water into the trough, when Alfie noticed the pig leaning heavily against the wall. It moved back and forth and from side to side as if it had an annoying itch between its shoulder blades that it couldn't quite scratch. It kept trying different positions, turning around, experimenting with other parts of the wall. Nothing seemed to satisfy it. Without stopping to consider what might happen if the pig was as bad-tempered as Makepeace and Widger, Alfie reached over and used his walking stick to rub the pig's back.

The creature was undoubtedly grateful. A grunt of satisfaction, and the pig leaned into the stick, inviting Alfie to scratch longer and harder. Its eyelashes fluttered and then – to Alfie's surprise – the pig's knees buckled and it sank to the ground with a sleepy sigh of satisfaction.

Alfie laughed. All his worries about the people in the woods and his fears about being sent back to London melted away as he watched the contented pig snoring. He'd been warned not to get attached to the animal, but it was impossible not to. Looking at it lying there in the autumn sunshine, huffing and grunting to itself, it looked so different from the dead things he'd seen in the butcher's shop, hanging by their heels on hooks, cut in half from snout to tail. It was impossible to think that this pig would go the same way.

After evening milking and supper, Auntie Bell said, "Maybe you'd like to pick some more blackberries tomorrow, eh? I could use them to make some nice bramble jelly. Fancy that, Alfie?"

Alfie had never tasted bramble jelly, but he said that he'd pick more blackberries for Auntie Bell whenever she wanted. The thought of blackberrying brought the strange people into his mind and all his earlier fears and worries came rushing back.

It must have shown on his face, because Auntie Bell frowned and said, "Poor birdie! Are you not feeling well? Tell you what, I shall give you a brick to warm the bed. Tis always nice and comforting when you're feeling peaky. And a cup of hot milk, eh? Sit yourself down until it's ready."

The sun was beginning to set, and Alfie sat on the window seat to watch the sky change. It was like the early mornings only in reverse. Once the sun had gone, there was a long period of twilight when the night animals began to stir as the light faded little by little and the stars came out. It was a magical time, in between the worlds of night and day, and he thought he'd never tire of watching it.

The blackout shutters on the top floor of the house were fitted inside the windows but the ones on the ground floor were fastened to the walls outside. Alfie could hear Ted at the front of the house bolting them shut. Soon the kitchen would be lit only with the dim, yellow glow of an oil lamp.

Alfie leaned his forehead against the glass and studied his reflection. His face looked see-through, like a ghost's. He stared, not quite recognizing his own features, feeling detached from the boy looking back at him.

He blinked slowly. Once. Twice. And suddenly, when he opened his eyes the second time, everything had changed. His transparent reflection had gone but another face was staring at him just inches away. Solid. Real. With eyes that were a vivid emerald green.

A stranger?

No... He'd seen him in the woods! It was the boy who'd been turned away from the hunt, smiling shyly at Alfie and raising a hand, his fingers splayed as if in greeting.

It was a shock, that was all. It wasn't exactly frightening. Surprise more than fear made Alfie cry out.

"Alfie dear!" said Auntie Bell. "Are you all right? Whatever happened?"

Alfie turned to face her. "There's someone out there!" He pointed back at the window. Auntie Bell crossed the kitchen floor and peered out into the dusk.

By the time she got there, Ted was outside, nodding at the pair of them through the glass before closing and bolting the blackout shutters. Then the window reflected only Alfie and Auntie Bell and the dim, yellow glow of the kitchen behind them.

"Hear something, did you?" asked Auntie Bell. Her voice was gentle and kind but she was giving him the Mr Moore look again. "Just Ted, that's all."

"Yes," said Alfie quickly. "It must have been. He made me jump!"

Auntie Bell smiled. "You'll most likely hear him again later, doing the rounds. He likes to make sure everything's shipshape before he turns in for the night. Drink your milk down and then let's get you up to bed. You're overtired, I dare say. Settling into a strange place is always hard. But a good night's sleep can work wonders. You'll be right as rain in the morning, I'm sure of it."

It wasn't his imagination, Alfie thought when he

was safely tucked into his bed. The boy had been there, right in front of him. He must have run away really fast when he heard Ted coming, otherwise the farmer would have seen him.

Alfie was just falling asleep when a question wreathed into his mind like a wisp of smoke.

If the boy had been there in the yard, why hadn't the dogs or the geese raised the alarm?

SCHOOL DAZE

Time behaved differently on Coombe Farm, Alfie decided, as he set off for school on Monday morning. It was hard to believe he'd only arrived in the village ten days ago. He felt not only that he'd always lived here, but that he always would. London and his mother seemed nothing more than a bad dream that he'd once had.

The village school was too small to accommodate both the Londoners and the local children at the same time. It had been decided amongst the grown-ups that the evacuees should be given a week to settle into their new homes before lessons started. After that, they would be taught by Miss Bottomley in the morning and the village children would attend lessons with their own teacher in the afternoon.

Alfie walked to school along the lanes. He could have taken the path down towards the beach and then walked upriver to the village, but it had rained heavily in the night and Auntie Bell said it wouldn't do to turn up covered in mud on his first day.

"They'll think I'm not looking after you properly. You must get there clean and tidy or I shall be hanging my head in shame." She smiled and straightened his collar.

Alfie had walked slowly when he left the farm. He felt safe there, with Auntie Bell and Ted and the dogs. Today he was going to have to face Billy Figgs and Violet and the rest of the children alone, without Auntie Bell there to protect him. As he neared the village, he grew more and more nervous.

By the time Alfie arrived, Miss Bottomley was already ringing the bell. He lined up with the other children and filed into the schoolroom.

Miss Bottomley had been Alfie's teacher back in London. There, she'd taught thirty children who were all the same age as Alfie, including Violet Davies. She now had fewer pupils, but they were such a mixture of ages and abilities that she didn't seem to know quite what to do with them. Alfie had never seen her look so flustered.

Billy Figgs had been in the year above Violet and Alfie. Now the three of them were ordered to sit next to each other in the back row. The nine other children were arranged in order of age and size. Jack, Violet's little brother, cried when Miss Bottomley told him to sit in the front.

"Buck up, boy!" she snapped, sounding uncannily like Lady Atherington.

Shocked, Jack fell silent. They all did.

Miss Bottomley was unusually short-tempered, Alfie noticed. In their old school, she'd usually start the day by reading them a story, a Greek myth or a tale of King Arthur and the Knights of the Round Table. If they'd been good, she'd end the day by letting them paint or draw. But today she began by having the whole group recite every single thing they knew by rote.

First it was currency.

"Twelve pennies to a shilling," they chanted in unison. "Twenty shillings to a pound. Four farthings in a penny. Two shillings in a florin. Two and six in half a crown. Five shillings in a crown."

Then they recited all the countries in the Empire and their capital cities. Next it was weights and measures. Lengths. Distances.

"Twenty-two yards one chain, ten chains one furlong, eight furlongs one mile."

Times tables were after that. Alfie was supposed

to know them by heart at his age but the numbers refused to lodge in his head, no matter how hard he tried. He mouthed them silently, expecting to be told off at any moment because Miss Bottomley always noticed when he was only miming. Today, thankfully, she seemed taken up with her own thoughts.

They had a short break in the middle of the morning. Miss Bottomley ushered the class outside and then closed the door behind them so she could have a cup of tea and a few minutes' peace.

Playtimes in London had always been a torment for Alfie. Ever since he could remember, he'd spent most of them trying and failing to keep out of Billy's way. Auntie Bell had given him a slice of cake wrapped in greaseproof paper, which Alfie was dying to eat. But Billy always snatched the treats anyone brought from home, so Alfie kept it tucked safely in his pocket. Although, actually, Alfie thought, fifteen minutes later, when Miss Bottomley rang the bell and they all trooped back inside, Billy was surprisingly quiet. Perhaps without Ned Smith and Stan Murphy at his side, and with Violet so taken up looking after Jack, he might not be the bully down here that he always had been in London?

After playtime, Miss Bottomley concentrated on the little ones, and gave the older children a set of mathematical problems to keep them busy until it was time to go home.

As always, the sums seemed to make no sense at all to Alfie.

"How long would it take a loaded donkey travelling at two and a quarter miles per hour to go five and a quarter miles?

"How long would it take the donkey to make two round trips?"

They might as well have asked him, *"If Betty buys six apples, five pears and an orange for two shillings and sixpence, how much does an elephant cost?"*

Alfie would rather have spent the morning trying to work out real problems. Like, why Lady Atherington always roosted in the rafters. Or what made Makepeace so bad-tempered? Or would he ever win the battle with the geese?

And – most importantly of all – why hadn't the dogs barked at the boy when he came into the yard?

The rest of the morning wore on slowly until the church clock finally struck twelve noon.

Home time!

When the evacuees headed out into the sunshine, the local children were already gathered outside, waiting to come in. They gave the evacuees nasty looks as Alfie and the others pushed their way through.

Joe Copper deliberately banged into Billy Figgs, who pushed him back so hard Joe almost fell over.

Alfie heard Miss Bottomley's voice from the schoolroom door.

"Stop that!" she protested.

Alfie didn't look back. He was already halfway up the lane.

The morning had passed without incident. Nothing nasty had happened. Neither had anything particularly nice. Later, when Auntie Bell asked him what he'd done at school, he was hard-pressed to recall anything.

The walk home, though? He could remember every single step of that.

HIDDEN LAUGHTER

It had taken Alfie over an hour to walk to school along the lanes, but Auntie Bell said the journey home would be quicker. If he took the more direct route along the river valley, he should get back to the farm by lunchtime. It didn't matter if he got muddy on the way, she said. Boots could be polished and clothes could be washed. So Alfie, instead of heading towards the bridge, turned towards the stile and a path that cut across a field of sheep before it came to the woods and the river that he could follow all the way down to the sea.

Knowing that this route was quicker, Alfie took his time. He'd find somewhere to stop before he got home, he thought. Then he could eat the now-squashed cake.

He sauntered through the trees, following the river's twists and turns. It was wide and shallow to begin with – knee-deep, perhaps – and he could see fish that were almost as long as his forearm darting across the stony bed and hiding in pools under tree roots along the bank. There was a bird, perched on a rock, bobbing its head up and down, dipping its beak into the water. It was slightly bigger than a sparrow, dark brown, almost black, with a white patch on its throat and chest that made it look as though it had a napkin tied around its neck. It dipped down again and then completely submerged itself in the water. Alfie could see it scurrying along the riverbed. After a few seconds, it emerged triumphant with something wriggling in its beak. Alfie watched it repeat the process once, twice, three times before moving slowly on.

Another twist. Another turn. He came to a place where the river deepened and narrowed so much that he could have jumped across it. But the far side was part of Lady Atherington's estate. There was a string of barbed wire and a sign nailed to the tree screaming:

KEEP OUT!

TRESPASSERS WILL BE PROSECUTED!

Alfie could have wriggled under the wire if he'd been really determined, yet he'd seen the size of Lady

Atherington's dogs. He didn't want to risk meeting them when they were off the lead. Besides, the water was flowing fast and furious just here, forcing itself between large grey, moss-covered rocks. If he slipped and fell, the strength of that rushing water would wash him away.

A little further on, the river slid over another massive slab of rock and then fell, tumbling for ten feet or more into a pool that looked big enough to swim in. Not that he'd ever learned how. Maybe he could teach himself when the weather was warm enough. Would he still be here by the summer? he wondered suddenly. The last war, the one old Mr Moore had fought in, had lasted four years. Would this one be the same? Or would it all be over by Christmas? What might happen to him then?

Thoughts of the future were too uncomfortable. Alfie pushed them out of his head and concentrated instead on the present.

There was another bird by the pool, a huge grey thing with spindly stilt-like legs standing as still as a statue. And then there was a flash of brilliant, jewel-like turquoise at the corner of his vision. It was gone by the time he turned his head. Another bird?

He'd remember the details and ask Auntie Bell about the birds later, he thought. He'd like to know what they were called. Maybe he could ask her about the different kinds of trees too. It would be nice to know the names of things.

At last, he emerged from the woods and saw the sea ahead. It was high tide now, the waves snapping and nipping at the foot of the cliffs, like Jake and Sam with the cows when they were bringing them in for milking. It was a clear, bright day and he could see the waterfall and the headland in the distance.

The stones.

He felt the pull of the place even from here. They were calling him.

That was silly! He had to be home for lunch, and that meant crossing the river and following the path back up through the woods to the farm. Giving himself a shake, Alfie jumped from one stepping stone to the other.

What was it that made him stop halfway across? Alfie had been ready to leap to the next stone when the hairs on the back of his neck prickled. A cold breeze had sprung up from nowhere. And he had the sudden feeling that he was no longer alone. He could feel the weight of someone's eyes on his skin.

He was being watched.

Alfie slowly turned full circle. The feeling of being observed grew stronger, but he couldn't see anyone.

"Who's there?" he called, his voice a little wobbly.
Silence.

"Come on out," he shouted, trying to make himself look big like he did with the geese. "Show yourself."

Nobody emerged from behind a rock. Nobody stepped out from behind a tree.

But he heard laughter. A giggle, not a snigger, immediately smothered. It reminded Alfie of Auntie Bell. Whoever was laughing was amused, not mocking. What were they finding so funny?

"Who's there?" he called.

The laugh came again. Whoever-it-was was giggling because Alfie couldn't see them.

A dim memory of London flashed through Alfie's brain. Children in the street, playing hide-and-seek. Laughing and giggling when they were found.

Was this a game, then? Was he supposed to find the giggler?

Close your eyes and count to ten, he thought. That's it.

So he did. And when his eyes were closed, he heard another suppressed laugh.

"One ..." he said, "two ..."

There was a rustle of leaves.

"... three ... four ..."

Feet, running up the path.

120

"… five … six."

More laughter.

"… seven … eight …"

Footsteps, heading up the hill. Towards the farm.

"… nine …"

Silence. Whoever it was had hidden themselves.

"… ten! Coming to get you!" yelled Alfie.

And he began to run

THE BOY WITH GREEN EYES

Alfie scooted up the path that zigzagged through the woods. He caught a snatch of laughter coming from behind a tree stump.

"Got you!" he said triumphantly, darting forwards. But when he reached it, no one was there.

A thud of footsteps ahead of him, higher up. Alfie ran towards the sound. Again, there was no one there. A flash of movement somewhere to his left. Out of the corner of his eye, he caught a glimpse of red hair. He turned his head. The boy had gone. Then the sound of his laughter gave away his position.

The boy was steadily working his way up the hill, leading Alfie along. Alfie, still not used to running up hills, was getting puffed out. It wasn't hide-and-seek, Alfie decided. It was chase. And he couldn't do it any more.

By then, he'd emerged from the woods and was on the clifftop. Alfie collapsed onto the grass.

"I give up," he called breathlessly. "You win."

And then the boy with green eyes, the boy who'd been turned away from the hunt, was suddenly there, raising his hand, fingers splayed in greeting before dropping down beside Alfie and stretching flat out on the grass, face to the sky, shading his eyes with his arm.

Alfie had never made a friend before, but he liked the idea of trying. He wasn't sure how you were supposed to start. How did other people manage it?

Maybe he should tell him his name. Was that the thing to do?

"Alfie," he said. "My name's Alfie."

The boy turned and lay on his side, propping himself up on one arm. He was frowning, regarding Alfie with curiosity but no comprehension. He opened his mouth, said something back. Alfie didn't understand his words, but thought from the tone that the boy had asked a question.

Hadn't he understood what Alfie had said? Didn't he speak English?

"Alfie," he said again. This time he thumped his chest and repeated, "Alfie. Alfie."

The boy's frown deepened as if he was concentrating.

"Effie," he said slowly. "Effie. Effie." He rolled the name around in his mouth, clearly finding the shape of it difficult to pronounce.

Alfie pointed at the boy and raised his eyebrows in a mute question.

The boy now thumped his own chest and said something that sounded to Alfie's ears like "Smidge".

There was definitely something strange in his accent, Alfie thought. He repeated the word, but couldn't mimic it exactly.

The boy laughed, shrugged and waggled his hand from side to side as if to say, "Not quite, but close enough."

And then he sat upright. Alfie did the same, and remembered the slab of squashed cake that was still in the pocket of his shorts.

Pulling it out, he unwrapped it and offered half to Smidge.

Grinning, muttering some strange word that might have meant "thanks", the boy took the crushed cake. As he did so, his fingers brushed against Alfie's palm.

Alfie found himself letting out a huge sigh of relief.

The boy was real. Solid flesh and blood, the same as him. Not a figment of his imagination after all.

Smidge made appreciative noises as he ate and then, when the last mouthful had been swallowed, he licked his fingers to get every single crumb.

Alfie wondered what he should say or do next. He had no idea how friendship was supposed to work, especially if you didn't speak the same language. He glanced at Smidge, a little perplexed. At the same time, Smidge shot a shy glance at Alfie. And, suddenly, Alfie realized that both of them wanted to be friends, but neither of them knew quite how to proceed. The silence lengthened. And lengthened. They looked at each other and shrugged helplessly at exactly the same moment. Both started to laugh. Smidge put his hand up and Alfie slapped it. No words needed to be said.

And then Auntie Bell's distant call drifted across the field towards them.

"Alfie! Alfie! Where are you, my birdie?"

Alfie stood up and waved at her.

"Here!" he called.

"Food's on the table!" she called back.

Alfie turned to say goodbye. But the boy had already gone.

ALIENS

"How was school today?" Auntie Bell asked Alfie as he tucked into his lunch. "Did you do anything nice?"

Alfie nodded vaguely and Auntie Bell smiled and ruffled his hair. As he chewed, she started to chatter about friends and neighbours and village news. Alfie barely heard a word. He was too busy thinking about Smidge.

The boy must have hidden the moment he'd heard Auntie Bell's voice. Just as he must have darted out of sight the other evening when Ted came to close the blackout shutters. The dogs hadn't barked but then they didn't bark at Alfie either. Perhaps Smidge had somehow made friends with them? As for the geese ... they'd already been shut in for the night.

Why didn't Smidge want to be seen?

He must be local, yet he didn't go to church on Sundays like everyone else. If he was the same age as Alfie – and he looked it – shouldn't he have been in school this afternoon? Was he playing truant? If that was the case, Alfie didn't want to get him into trouble.

No ... there was more to it than that. The boy's unbrushed hair, his clothes, so different from anything Alfie had ever seen anyone wearing. Maybe there was something else going on, something Alfie couldn't understand. He chomped through his meal, turning the problem over and over in his mind.

Perhaps it was something to do with Smidge not speaking English?

Alfie had grown up in London, where all kinds of people from all sorts of countries rubbed shoulders with each other. He could walk down his street on any day of the week and hear people talking in at least a dozen different languages. Everyone had seemed to get along, more or less, until all the talk of war started. And then Mr and Mrs Licata, the Italians who ran the ice-cream shop on the main road, had had a brick through their window. The Browns – Germans who'd lived in the house opposite Alfie for as long as he could remember – were accused of being enemy aliens. A van had come and they'd been forced to get into it and, when Alfie asked where they were going, his mother said they were being taken off to a camp. Alfie had pictured tents and cheerful sing-songs around a roaring campfire – the kind of things that children did in the adventure books he sometimes borrowed from the library.

"Then why do they look sad?" he'd asked.

And she'd snapped back that it wasn't that sort of camp. There had been something in her voice that scared him, so he didn't ask any more.

He didn't want to hear that same bitter ring in Auntie Bell's voice. He didn't want to see that same suspicious, sour look on her face.

Grown-ups were funny about foreigners these days. Instinct told him that it would be best if he kept quiet about his new friend.

"MY NEW HOME"

The next day at school, Miss Bottomley made the older children compose an essay on "My New Home" while she helped the little ones with their reading and writing.

For Alfie, school was mostly something to be endured rather than enjoyed. If it wasn't mathematical problems making him feel stupid, it was the other children giving him the cold shoulder. It wasn't that they disliked Alfie, or that he'd done anything to upset them. His only crime was getting picked on by Billy Figgs. No one wanted to make friends with Alfie for fear of being treated the same.

The one thing Alfie did enjoy at school was writing. Stories, poems, accounts of historical events – anything that carried him to a different time and place. It was like capturing daydreams with words, giving form and substance to the pictures in his head.

A lot of things were in short supply with the war on and they were only allowed one sheet of paper each for their essay. Alfie, who had a lot to say about the farm and the animals, wrote in his tiniest handwriting so he could fit it all in. He wrote about the cows and Blossom and Makepeace and the geese and Lady Atherington, who still pecked him every morning and he didn't know why (although he had the sense not to mention the hen by name). He described how the pig grunted "hello" at him every time he crossed the yard and how it loved having its back scratched with the walking stick he used to defend himself from the geese. He wrote about Jake and Sam and about how he wasn't supposed to make a fuss of them, but how the dogs didn't seem to know that and always ran over to him to be patted whenever he appeared in the yard. Alfie was so absorbed he was unaware that either side of him Violet Davies and Billy Figgs were struggling to manage even a single paragraph.

When the essays were gathered in at the end of the morning, Miss Bottomley gave Alfie one of her rare smiles. She despaired of him ever learning his times tables, yet the child certainly knew how to write. If only there was a practical use for such a skill! She couldn't imagine what would become of a dreamer like Alfie in later life.

When she read their essays, Miss Bottomley became painfully aware that apart from Alfie, her older pupils were struggling with homesickness every bit as much as the younger children. The following week she set the little ones some handwriting exercises so she could have a quiet word with the bigger children when she handed their work back.

To Violet, Miss Bottomley said, with a sympathetic look, "Being on one's best behaviour all the time can be terribly wearing, can't it? I'm sure it will get easier with time."

To Carrie and Claire, she said, "Being away from family is awfully hard. At least you have each other. Cling tightly to that."

To Billy: "It sounds like frightfully hard work. We all have to do our bit during this miserable war, though. I dare say you'll get used to it."

For some reason, Miss Bottomley didn't give Alfie his essay back – he could see she was still holding it when she returned to the front of the class. Had she forgotten him?

She turned to face the children and smiled. And

then, to Alfie's utter horror, she held up his essay and declared in a loud voice that it was a "fine piece of writing" and "something to be very proud of".

And then she read it out. Slowly. Word by word. Miss Bottomley had never done anything like that before. Any remarks on Alfie's work were usually at the bottom of the page in neat, sloping letters. *Good work* if it was a story. *See me* if it was Maths. What on earth did she think she was doing?

Alfie – who hated being the centre of attention – was overcome with embarrassment. And still his suffering wasn't over. When she reached the end of the essay, she smiled at him and said, "I'm most impressed that you attempted to milk a cow! Perhaps we could all come and visit one day, and Mrs Hartland could give us a demonstration?"

Alfie squirmed in his seat and said nothing. The thought of the other children rampaging around the farm horrified him. They wouldn't see magic, he thought. They'd see muck. He didn't want them there. It was his special place and he didn't want to share it.

The silence was broken by Violet, leaning towards Alfie and saying, "Ain't you scared of them cows?"

She was looking at him in the way she had when he'd arrived in the village riding on Blossom's back, as if she was impressed.

Before Alfie could reply, Billy Figgs sniggered loudly from the seat beside him.

"Alfie Wright touched a cow's bosoms!" he announced.

The schoolroom erupted into giggles. For a moment, Violet didn't join in. Then Billy stared at her and repeated his joke pointedly. After a second's pause, she laughed.

It took Miss Bottomley several minutes to calm the class.

"You're all being very, very silly," she said when they'd finally settled.

"We was just having a bit of fun, Miss," grumbled Billy.

"Fun?" Miss Bottomley said "Well, I'm not laughing. And neither is Alfie. I don't want to hear another word out of you this morning, Billy Figgs."

Although silence reigned, Alfie knew this wouldn't be the end of it. On one side, Billy was glaring at him furiously. On the other, Violet gave him a sideways look, bit her lip and flushed scarlet.

KINGFISHER BLUE

In the days and weeks that followed, relations between the village children and the evacuees grew more and more strained.

Alfie didn't get involved. He saw the local kids in church on Sundays but he was always with Auntie Bell and Ted. After the service, when Auntie Bell finished chatting with her friends and exchanging the latest news on the war, they always had to get back to the farm. The only other time Alfie crossed paths with Joe and the rest of them was at noon each day when they were there outside, lined up to go into the schoolroom when the evacuees finished for the morning.

With each day that passed, Alfie noticed the growing enmity between the two groups. First, there was muttering as they passed each other. Then mumbled whispers became words. The vague sense of animosity that had centred around Billy Figgs and Joe Copper became more general. It was still only pushing and shoving and name-calling, yet it was getting worse.

Alfie wanted nothing to do with it. The moment the evacuees were released from school, he would leave the village as fast as he could, half walking, half running, only slowing down when he'd crossed the field and reached the cover of the woods.

And every day, without fail, somewhere along the path that ran beside the river, Smidge would fall into step beside him and keep Alfie company until he reached the farm.

Alfie never heard Smidge coming. One minute he'd be alone, and the next there would be a shift of light and air, the landscape would subtly rearrange itself, and the boy would appear, green eyes sparkling, red hair glowing in the sunlight, looking so pleased to see Alfie that thoughts of school and Billy and Joe and all the rest of the children vanished from Alfie's mind.

The experience of having a friend to play with was dizzying. They might not speak the same language, but Alfie found that he and Smidge didn't really need to. They understood each other somehow. They were relaxed in each other's company. Who needed any more than that?

Alfie had learned from Auntie Bell that the tree with the smooth, grey bark was a beech. The one that looked as if it had been raked all over with a giant fork was an oak. The small bird with the white bib was called a dipper. Smidge had a different name for it that Alfie couldn't pronounce. The huge grey bird was a heron. Smidge called it a *can-nut.* Or something like that. Alfie couldn't quite get his mouth around that, either. Mind you, Smidge had the same problem with English. Sometimes their mistakes in each other's languages made both boys snort with laughter.

In fact, they did more laughing than talking. One afternoon, Alfie taught Smidge the hand-slapping game that he'd seen other children play at breaktime. They had reached the beach by then and it was almost time to head back up through the woods to the farm, but first Alfie said, "Stand there, Smidge." He put his hands on the boy's shoulders to root him to the spot and then stepped back. Putting his palms together, Alfie pointed his fingers towards Smidge's chest and indicated that Smidge should do the same.

When the ends of the boys' fingers were touching Alfie said, "My turn first. One ... two ... three."

As quickly as he could, Alfie tried to slap the backs of Smidge's hands. Smidge instinctively jerked them away and all Alfie hit was empty air.

Smidge was looking at Alfie uncertainly.

"It's a game," said Alfie, smiling. "You –" pointing at Smidge – "hit –" gesturing a slap – "Alfie –" patting his own chest. Alfie grinned again, and put his hands back together.

"Your turn," he said.

It took a moment for Smidge to understand, and then he complied, pressing his palms together and touching fingers with Alfie.

"Effie. Un ... ooo ... ree."

And then Smidge moved so quickly that Alfie had no time to react. Smidge slapped the back of Alfie's hands and then whooped in triumph.

Alfie took his turn, but Smidge was so fast! He beat Alfie time and time again. Alfie only managed to land one or two slaps on Smidge and he suspected that was because Smidge had deliberately let him.

How long they played that game, Alfie wasn't sure. They'd laughed until they were both weak from it.

By the time he got back to the farm, his hands were tingling and he had a great big grin on his face. If this was what having a friend felt like, Alfie thought, it was nice.

Sometimes they didn't talk or play games. They just sat in companionable silence watching the sea, or the birds. The flash of brilliant turquoise that Alfie had seen the first time he'd walked along the river, and that Auntie Bell had informed him was probably a kingfisher, hadn't appeared again. It was a shame. He'd like to know Smidge's name for it.

So, one Friday afternoon, Alfie finally said, "You ... Smidge –" pointing to the boy – "see –" indicating his eyes – "bird?" He put his wrists together and fluttered his hands like birds' wings. And then he pointed to his pullover, which was a much duller colour than the bird had been, yet was at least blue. "This colour?" And then he wobbled his hand to indicate, "Sort of."

Smidge frowned in earnest concentration as Alfie spelled out his question in signs and gestures. There was a brief pause while he thought. And then he smiled, nodded and said, "Ya ... Effie ... Fim, fim." And he waved a hand, indicating that Alfie should follow.

Noiselessly, Smidge led Alfie to the place where the river narrowed and, without a backward glance, leapt across to the other side.

Alfie felt a brief moment of alarm. He'd been warned not to set foot on Lady Atherington's land without permission. What about her dogs? Yet the string of barbed wire had been removed and the sign nailed to the tree had gone too. Maybe Lady Atherington had changed her mind about trespassers?

Smidge was already disappearing into the trees and the desire to follow him was just too strong to resist. Alfie jumped over and ran to catch up with his friend.

Smidge led Alfie along the river through a carpet of blue flowers until they neared the pool where Alfie had seen the heron.

Suddenly Smidge put a finger to his lips and a hand on Alfie's arm. He bent low and gestured for Alfie to do the same. He crept, silent as a ghost, closer to the water. Then stopped dead. When Alfie caught him up, he pointed. There was a small hole in the opposite bank. As they watched, a kingfisher emerged from it, perching on a branch, orange and turquoise blue, before diving suddenly into the pool. Moments later, it emerged with a silver fish in its beak that it carried back into the hole. There was faint noise coming from inside, hard to make out over the sound of the river, but possibly cheeping. Alfie looked at Smidge enquiringly.

Smidge did the same hand gesture that Alfie had to indicate wings. Then he held his thumb and forefinger together to indicate something very small.

Small birds? Chicks! thought Alfie. That must be what Smidge meant.

Sparrows nested under the eaves of Alfie's house in London every spring, noisy things, screaming for food, scrapping and arguing like children in the street.

It was autumn now, not spring. Maybe kingfishers nested at a different time of year? Because that hole certainly seemed to be the kingfishers' nest. And the way the bird came out again and dived to catch more fish suggested there were hungry chicks in there.

The two boys watched until Alfie's stomach rumbled loudly and he realized that he was going to be late for lunch.

"Got to go!" he said.

He turned and ran back to where the river narrowed, jumped across and hurried back to Coombe Farm, ready with apologies for keeping Auntie Bell and Ted waiting.

But when he got home, Auntie Bell was only just beginning to lay the table.

THE LADY
ATHERINGTON PROBLEM

Eggs, thought Alfie, his eyes snapping open. It was all to do with eggs.

Watching the kingfisher with Smidge had somehow got mixed up with the memory of sparrows nesting in the eaves when he lived in London. Birds had fluttered through his dreams that night. By the time he woke on Saturday, he realized that Lady Atherington pecked him every morning because he was taking her eggs. No wonder she got so cross! She probably saw it as stealing. The only real surprise was that the rest of the hens were so relaxed about it.

Alfie got out of bed and started pulling on his clothes. After milking, he'd ask Auntie Bell if he could go to the beach, he thought. He'd had an idea. If he could find some pebbles that were the same size and shape as a chicken's egg, then maybe it would solve the problem of Lady Atherington?

The tide was ebbing when Alfie reached the beach. He found a stone that was the right size almost immediately, but if his plan was to work he'd probably need more than one. Finding another was less easy. They were all too big or too small or too lumpy.

Alfie was so preoccupied with his task that he didn't notice the change in light and temperature at first. But he did notice that the sea – which had been almost lapping at his feet – had suddenly retreated further, exposing the rocks and the deep channels that ran between them. He stood for a moment, watching a crab scuttle sideways across the bottom of a rock pool.

And then he noticed Smidge standing some distance away, perfectly motionless, bare-chested, bare-legged, knee-deep in water, a spear in his hand.

Up until now, Alfie had only seen Smidge when he was looking for Alfie, seeking him out. Now Alfie had caught Smidge unawares, when he was concentrating on something else.

Alfie almost called out to him, then wondered if

he shouldn't interrupt. Maybe he should go home and leave Smidge to whatever he was doing?

Yet there was something fascinating about someone who could stand so still. Didn't Smidge feel the cold? A stiff breeze was coming off the sea now and that water must be freezing! What was Smidge *doing*?

Alfie wanted to go closer but didn't dare break the spell. Instead, he stayed where he was, higher up the beach, hands in pockets, watching.

When it came, the movement was so quick that if Alfie had blinked, he would have missed it: the spear, thrust into the water and pulled out; a fish the length of Smidge's forearm thrashing on the end of it. Its struggle for life was so violent that it threw the boy off balance. He tried to climb out of the pool but lost his footing on the seaweed-slippery rocks and fell. Spear and fish flew out of his hand. Alfie heard the crack of the haft breaking and Smidge's cry of frustration. The fish was flipping, jerking, trying to get itself back to the sea.

Without thinking, Alfie ran.

He'd never touched a live fish before. His mother cooked herrings for tea sometimes, glass-eyed, stiff, stinky things a million miles away from this desperate, thrashing creature. When he reached Smidge, Alfie grabbed the fish's tail but it was hard to keep hold of it. Then Smidge was there, back on his feet, bringing a stone down on the fish's head, killing it swiftly and cleanly. Blood ran over the rock, into the water.

Smidge looked fiercely delighted. He nodded thanks at Alfie but didn't waste breath on words. Instead, taking the spearhead, he gutted the fish, throwing its head and innards towards the waiting gulls. Then he grinned and held the fish out. He pointed at Alfie, then pointed at himself, and mimed eating by holding the fish to his mouth and pretending to chomp along it.

"Oh!" said Alfie. "You want to share it?"

It would be rude to refuse, though the idea of eating a raw fish wasn't appealing. Still, Alfie had long been taught to mind his manners, so he nodded politely, rubbing his tummy to indicate that he was hungry.

Smidge jerked his head sideways, eyebrows raised, turned away from the water and started walking up the beach. Alfie fell into step beside him.

They stopped at the foot of the cliffs, where successive high tides had deposited a line of driftwood. There was no rubbish, though. No fishing net, no jars, no tin cans. It was nicer today. Cleaner.

Smidge set the fish down on the stones and began searching for something in the pouch he wore tied around his waist. He pulled out what looked like a handful of dried moss and a pair of stones. Squatting down on his haunches, he arranged the moss on the pebbles then balanced a few twigs around the pile.

Smidge, Alfie realized, was trying to light a fire to roast the fish over. Smidge struck the two stones together, but his hands were cold and clumsy and, try as he might, he couldn't get a spark.

He was near to weeping with frustration when Alfie thought of his magnifying glass.

That could be used to start a fire! He'd discovered it once, outside his house. He'd been playing alone, as always. The sunlight had shone through his magnifying glass and Alfie had focussed a beam on a pile of dry leaves that – to his surprise – had started to smoulder. Old Mr Moore had come along then and, when he'd seen the wisp of smoke, he'd started to cry for some reason, great sobs that made him shake.

Alfie was so horrified to have upset the old man that he'd never tried to make it happen again. Poor old Mr Moore was far away now, though. He wouldn't be bothered by anything Alfie did.

"Let me have a go," said Alfie, tapping his own chest.

He pulled the magnifying glass from his pocket, showed it briefly to Smidge, who looked utterly mystified, and then focussed the sunlight into a narrow beam on the moss. It wasn't too long before the moss started to smoulder.

Smidge gave a cry of amazement and, for a moment, looked almost afraid, as if Alfie had performed some sort of dark magic. Smidge was so taken aback by Alfie's feat it took him a few seconds to get back to the task in hand. Then he seemed to make a decision. He smiled, clapped a friendly hand on Alfie's shoulder and started to fuel the fire with larger twigs and bits of wood until he had a good blaze going. When Smidge was satisfied, he spiked the fish on to a stick and suspended it over the fire. Then he pointed at the magnifying glass as if asking for a closer look.

Alfie held it out to him but Smidge seemed reluctant to touch it.

"It's all right," said Alfie. "It won't hurt you. Take it."

Smidge reached out a single finger and pressed it against the glass tentatively as if scared it might burn him. When it didn't, his confidence grew. Gingerly, he took the magnifying glass from Alfie, cupping it in both hands and looking at it in wonder, as if it was more precious than the crown jewels.

After a while, Alfie gestured at Smidge's spearhead.

"Can I have a look?" he said, holding out a hand, and Smidge obliged.

The two boys sat side by side, Alfie feeling the sharpness of the stone blade, marvelling at the skill that had gone into creating it. It wasn't the kind of thing you could buy in a shop, Alfie thought. So how had Smidge got hold of it? He suddenly remembered the blacksmith, hitting red-hot iron with a hammer, shaping it into a horseshoe. His eyes narrowed thoughtfully.

"Did you make this?" he asked suddenly.

Smidge looked puzzled, so Alfie mimed.

"You, Smidge –" he pointed at the boy's chest – "make..." He couldn't think how to get the word across and ended up miming Auntie Bell shaping a bread roll. "Smidge make..." he said again, "this?" holding up the spearhead.

Smidge nodded enthusiastically. Laying the magnifying glass down gently in his lap, he took back the spearhead, picked up a pebble from the beach and showed Alfie that he'd chipped away at a stone, little by little, until he'd got it just right.

"That's clever!"

Smidge didn't understand the words, but Alfie's admiration was so obvious it made the boy grin. He picked up the magnifying glass again and then copied the hand gestures Alfie had made.

"Effie ... mek ... dis?"

"No!"

Alfie laughed at the thought. He remembered finding it. He'd been small – maybe three or four years old – and had been digging in the patch of dirt in the back yard with a spoon he'd taken from the kitchen drawer. He'd bent the handle, he remembered suddenly. His mother had been furious. He performed an elaborate mime of the scene for Smidge, scratching away at the ground, his spoon hitting something hard, unearthing the magnifying glass.

Smidge looked at it with renewed awe and wonder as if it was something holy. Sacred. Reluctantly, he offered it back to Alfie.

The magnifying glass was Alfie's most precious possession. His favourite thing, the object he always carried in his pocket. And yet here was Smidge, fishing to feed himself, needing to make a fire to eat…

"No," said Alfie, raising his hand and batting it away. "You keep it. It's a present."

When the meaning of Alfie's gesture sunk in, Smidge clutched the gift to his chest and opened his mouth but no words emerged. He seemed to be thinking hard. And then an idea came to him. He held out the spearhead and offered it to Alfie.

"You want to give that to me? A swap? Cor! Thanks, Smidge."

Deal done, the fish was ready to eat. Having no plates or knives or forks, they ate it with their fingers.

Alfie had never tasted anything so delicious.

MATTERS OF
LIFE AND DEATH

Watching Smidge catch the fish, lighting the fire and cooking it had all been so exciting that the problem of Lady Atherington had been pushed out of Alfie's head. It wasn't until he was getting dressed the following morning that he remembered the pebble in his pocket.

After milking, Alfie went to the small barn as usual. Instead of dislodging Lady Atherington with the walking stick, he climbed the ladder with a pebble concealed in his left hand. The bird was as furiously indignant as she was every morning, fluffing up her speckled feathers and preparing for an all-out attack. Quickly, Alfie slid his hand under her belly and swapped the pebble for the egg.

The look on Lady Atherington's face as he started back down the ladder almost made Alfie fall off. The hen blinked, realized that there was still something egg-shaped underneath her, and gave Alfie a puzzled, penetrating stare as if somehow suspecting he'd played a trick. Then she emitted a throaty, broody cluck and settled back down.

Later, when Alfie told Auntie Bell what he'd done, she said, "You clever thing! I should never have thought of it. I said we'd turn you into a proper country lad, didn't I?"

The bubble of happiness that had started to grow inside Alfie's chest as he left London continued to swell. September had melted into October and, as the month wore on, the warm weather gave way to bouts of heavy rain. Alfie was aware that the days were getting shorter, the nights steadily lengthening. One morning, the air was so cold and crisp his breath billowed in clouds in front of him on the way to school.

And yet every afternoon, when Alfie walked home and Smidge fell into step beside him, the sun came out and stayed out until he arrived home for lunch.

Alfie knew the grown-ups were worried about the war. Every night he could hear Auntie Bell and Ted talking in the kitchen long after he'd gone to bed.

And on Sundays, the conversations in the graveyard after church had grown quieter and more anxious. Poland had really copped it, the grown-ups said. The country had been attacked by both the Germans and the Russians and, after a courageous fight, Poland had finally surrendered. There was talk about the Germans invading Britain and the threat of big cities like London being bombed to smithereens. And there was his mother, right in the middle of it all. Alfie knew he should be worried sick about her, and yet, somehow, his mother and London and the whole war felt distant and unreal. Even though he saw army planes going over sometimes, they seemed to belong to a different world and another time – one that was entirely unconnected to him.

Then, one evening, Ted came in for supper and said dully, "Any day now, I reckon." He was looking at Auntie Bell with a face so grim that Alfie felt fear clutch at his throat. Was the threatened invasion about to start?

The huge, solid slab of a farmer turned away abruptly, and busied himself throwing an extra log on the already blazing fire.

Alarmed, Alfie glanced at Auntie Bell, wondering if he dared ask what was going on.

Seeing Alfie's fear, Auntie Bell said softly, "Pig

killing day will soon be here. Nothing for you to worry about, Alfie. We'll do it while you're at school."

Alfie's stomach heaved. He felt sick. Big boys weren't supposed to cry, his mother always said. And yet the tears were rising.

Alfie remembered Auntie Bell saying that her husband Bill used to cry for a week before killing the pig. Was Ted going to do the same? He had his back to them now, but Alfie heard the young man sniff and saw him rub his eyes.

If boys weren't supposed to cry, then men definitely weren't allowed. Alfie had never seen a man in tears, apart from old Mr Moore sometimes, and people tutted at that and said it was another sign he wasn't right in the head.

"We all have to eat, my birdie. Tis just the way life is," said Auntie Bell gently. She was looking at the floor and Alfie didn't know if she was talking to Ted or him. "Some things have to die so that others can live."

It was true. Alfie knew that. Hadn't he helped Smidge kill that fish? Hadn't he happily shared it with him? And yet...

"It doesn't seem very fair," he said.

Auntie Bell turned towards him. "No, I don't suppose it does at your age, especially coming from a city, and not having grown up with it the way people do around here. Mother Nature is a beautiful thing, but she can be very cruel. Here on the farm ... we do our best to soften it, when we can. We treat our animals well, we give them good lives and when tis time for them to go, we kill them quick and clean so they don't suffer. Tis the way God designed the world. You shall get used to it, I expect."

Alfie didn't say anything, but he didn't think he ever would. He went to bed that night feeling ill at the thought of what was going to happen to the pig. For weeks it had grunted a greeting at him every time he went past the sty. And sometimes, when it caught sight of Alfie with his walking stick, it hooked its front trotters over the door, standing on its back legs like a dog, asking for him to come and give it a scratch. And Alfie could never say no.

But the next day, when he went to let the birds out, he avoided the sty by taking the long way around the yard. He could hardly bear the feeling that he was betraying the pig somehow, pretending to be its friend, yet knowing its fate and doing nothing to prevent it. The thought of eating the creature revolted him. And yet he knew, deep down, that, when it came to it, he probably wouldn't be able to resist the roast pork and crackling, any more than Ted and his father had.

"Some things have to die so that others can live,"

Auntie Bell had said. The words banged around inside Alfie's head all that day, and, when he climbed the stairs to the box room for bed, they were still circling in his mind like birds of prey. When sleep started creeping up on him, thoughts of the pig somehow became all muddled up with old Mr Moore and his young soldier friends and the vicar's sermons every Sunday about how, during a war, lives must be sacrificed for the greater good. When Alfie finally slept, he dreamed about Smidge, seeing, over and over again, the boy bringing the stone down on the fish's head. And its blood running over the rock and into the sea.

PART II

The Seer was perplexed. She had fasted. And she had prayed and waited. Waited and prayed. And yet the Goddess had sent no vision.

There was muttering amongst the clan. The hunters were becoming impatient. The days were shortening but she still could not give them word of what they were to hunt. In past years, before the circle was completed, she had been able to say by now: You must take a stag. A boar. A horse.

They must capture, not kill the animal. Capture it without making a mark on its body. Such feats required great skill and cunning. They required planning.

Once captured, the animal needed to be kept alive until Midwinter. As the last sliver of the sun descended into the sea on Midwinter's night, it would be sacrificed, its blood spilled, its carcass burned, its bones buried, to feed Mother Earth and restore her strength. Only then could the year turn. Only then would the sun be able to rise once more and drive away the Darkness.

Yet this year, no visions had come. No animal had

haunted her dreams at night or run through her thoughts during the day. The only creature that entered her mind was the foundling boy, Smidge. Always Smidge.

And though Starver said different, she knew it was not possible... No ... she refused to believe it. It simply could not be that the Goddess meant them to sacrifice a child.

STICKS AND STONES

The pig's imminent slaughter made Alfie look at the world differently. When he walked to and from school that week, he felt as though everything had slipped sideways. Places, objects all looked the same as they always had, but now there seemed to be something darker lurking just beneath the surface. He started to notice things he hadn't before. Hidden dangers. Unseen cruelty. Feathers on the path that he might have ignored a week ago now told the story of a bird that had been killed and eaten. The night noises of owls and foxes were full of menace. And those occasional shrieks of mice or voles that pierced the night... He knew now they were screams of panic and pain that were cut short as their little lives ended.

And something between him and Smidge was different too.

One afternoon, Alfie had noticed as soon as Smidge joined him that the boy was tense and edgy. His smile, when he fell into step beside Alfie, looked forced. As they strolled along the riverbank, Smidge almost leapt out of his skin at a sudden noise behind them. It was a bird, that was all. A wood pigeon, crashing clumsily from one branch to another and yet Smidge paled as though he was afraid.

The next day, Smidge didn't appear as usual when Alfie entered the woods. He followed the path expecting the boy to join him at any moment, yet it wasn't until Alfie reached the place where the river fell into the deep pool that he finally saw his friend. Smidge was sitting on a rock looking into the water and hadn't heard him coming. When Alfie called his name, Smidge turned. He smiled quickly, but Alfie had seen the look of terrible sadness on his face.

It wasn't just that Smidge seemed unhappy. He couldn't settle to any of the things they usually did. The week before, they'd spent long periods just sitting side by side, watching the kingfishers feeding their chicks, and dragonflies dancing across the water. They'd sat on the beach throwing pebbles at targets and skimming flat stones across the calm sea. Now

Smidge seemed restless. Itchy. As if he was expecting something bad to happen at any moment.

On Friday afternoon, Smidge wasn't there again when Alfie entered the woods and there was no sign of him as he walked along beside the river. By the time he reached the beach, Alfie was seriously worried. He kept calling Smidge's name but there was no reply. He was about to give up and go back home to the farm when there was a change in light and he noticed a hunched figure crouched down at the foot of the cliffs up ahead.

"Smidge?" he called again.

The figure turned, and – yes – it was his friend. Smidge was busy with something and though he jerked his head, indicating that Alfie should join him, he didn't raise a hand or smile in greeting. Was he gutting a fish? Alfie wondered. Or making a fire? Alfie approached, keen to find out.

Smidge had a large flat slab of driftwood in one hand and the magnifying glass in the other. Angling it towards the sun he waited for the wood to smoulder.

Yes, he was starting a fire, Alfie thought as he watched. But no, each time the wood darkened, Smidge moved the magnifying glass little by little, until he'd made a black, charred line. Sudden realization made Alfie gasp. Smidge was using the beam of light like a pencil! He was drawing with sunlight!

Alfie watched, fascinated as the first line was slowly followed by another. And another. Gradually the image of a creature with spindly legs and branch-like horns on its head, galloping with legs outstretched as if running for its life, appeared on the wood. Alfie was overawed and Smidge wasn't finished yet. Next he drew a stick-thin figure, running after the animal, spear in hand.

Then Smidge gently laid down the magnifying glass and looked at Alfie nervously, as if worried about what he might think.

"That's so clever!" Alfie said. "You're amazing, Smidge!"

A look of relief spread across the boy's face.

Alfie realized then that it wasn't simply that he liked Smidge; he *admired* him. Smidge wasn't just fun to be with; he was clever and resourceful. He had ingenious ways of doing things. He could be an inventor when he grew up, Alfie thought. Or an artist, or something.

"Is that you?" Alfie said, pointing to the human figure. "Is this Smidge?"

Smidge nodded. "Smidge," he said. "Smidge..." Then he pointed to the animal and said another word that Alfie didn't understand. He mimed plunging a spear into something then rubbed his tummy and made chewing noises to show that the animal was good to eat.

Alfie was thoughtful for a moment or two. He knew Smidge didn't go to church or school and was never seen in the village, so he couldn't buy food from the shop. The boy had to hunt to feed himself. Alfie already knew Smidge could kill a fish, but a large animal? That felt sort of different, somehow.

For the first time, Alfie looked closely at what Smidge was wearing. It was cold that day and he had on a sort of jacket with a hood that Alfie hadn't seen before. He hadn't thought much about Smidge's strange clothes, but now he realized that nothing the boy wore was knitted from wool or cut from woven cloth. This new garment was stitched together from some sort of animal hide. The hair was still clearly visible.

A dreadful thought occurred to Alfie. Smidge's jacket was the same reddish-brown colour as Auntie Bell's cows. Smidge couldn't have killed one of them, could he? Was such a thing even possible with a spear? He touched Smidge's sleeve and made the mooing noise of a cow, raising his eyebrows to show it was a question.

Smidge frowned and shook his head.

Alfie made the noise of a sheep instead.

Another shake of the head.

Alfie barked like a dog.

"Nah!" said Smidge, laughing and waving his hand to indicate that it wasn't any of those. And then he made the sound of a horse neighing.

"Crikey!" said Alfie. If Smidge was trying to lie low, then killing and skinning a horse was no better than doing it to a cow. The owner would be furious! But Alfie didn't know how to tell Smidge that, so he said nothing. It was time for him to get back to the farm in any case, he thought. He'd been watching Smidge make the picture for ages.

"I ought to go," Alfie said, getting to his feet. Smidge did the same.

Alfie raised his hand in the air to say farewell. Today, at any rate, Smidge seemed happy. Maybe Alfie had imagined the jittery mood?

When Smidge slapped Alfie's palm with his own, the sleeve of his jacket slipped back.

There was a pattern of bruises on Smidge's arm. A pattern that Alfie had once seen on his own flesh after a close encounter with Billy Figgs' father. Alfie looked closer and knew with a chill prickle of alarm that the marks had been left by someone's fingers. Not long ago, someone had grabbed Smidge and held him so tightly they'd left red and purple marks on his skin.

PEACE AND GOODWILL

Alfie walked home feeling horribly unsettled. And things only got worse when he reached Coombe Farm.

The sty was empty.

Auntie Bell had been true to her word and slaughtered the pig while Alfie was safely at school. He was relieved not to have seen or heard the killing but he felt like a coward too. And a traitor. He hadn't even tried to save the pig. Then, on the beach, he'd seen Smidge's arm and the bruises and had no idea how to ask him who'd done it and so he'd simply walked away. Alfie felt helpless. Powerless. Useless.

And that evening, Ted was equally miserable, red-eyed and silent. Even Auntie Bell's chatter slowed and eventually dried up altogether.

When Alfie went to bed that night, he found it hard

to get to sleep. His mind was full of Auntie Bell's words again: *Some things have to die so that others can live.* Eventually, he drifted off, but his sleep was shallow, and horrible, restless dreams churned through his mind.

Alfie often saw Smidge on a Saturday. Once his farm chores were done, he'd take himself off for a walk down to the beach or through the woods along the river, and Smidge would invariably join him somewhere along the way. On this particular Saturday, perhaps sensing Alfie's dark mood, Auntie Bell kept finding jobs for him to do on the farm. The small barn needed mucking out; all the straw in the nesting boxes needed replacing. The tool shed needed tidying; she needed help churning the butter and making the bread. Alfie didn't see Smidge at all that day.

There was trouble in the village that same afternoon between the evacuees and the local children. It started as a game of Tommies and Jerries, Joe Copper leading his army against Billy Figgs'.

The first Alfie knew of it was when they went to church the following morning.

"Outrageous behaviour!" Lady Atherington tutted as she tied her dogs up to the church gate. Falling into step beside Auntie Bell as they walked up the path towards the church she added, "Joe Copper and that frightful evacuee – what's his name? Billy, I believe? They were running wild!"

It seemed that the game had turned into an all-out fight with children hunkered down behind gravestones hurling stones at each other and Billy and Joe having a fist fight in the church porch.

"They were behaving like savages!" exclaimed Her Ladyship. "It was disgraceful. If I'd known what was going on, I'd have set the dogs on them. The vicar needs to bang their heads together."

When they went into church, Alfie could see that Claire Thompson had a cut on her forehead and Carrie had the smudge of a bruise across her cheek. Violet had scratch marks all down one arm. Billy Figgs had a proper shiner and could barely see out of his blackened, swollen right eye. The village children had suffered similar injuries. Joe Copper had a cut lip and his nose was red as if he'd been thumped in the face. Both sides were glaring at each other until Alfie walked in. And then all their eyes turned to him, looking resentfully at the one child who hadn't taken part in the battle, the one child who wasn't in trouble.

After hymns and prayers, the vicar gave a long, long, lecture from the pulpit about the need for unity and pulling together.

"This war will never be won if we as a people are

divided. We must all play our part, from the most senior to the very youngest amongst us."

Alfie had escaped the children's fight, but he couldn't evade the vicar's solution to their war. Reverend Braithwaite was determined to build bridges, he said. The nativity he'd proposed as an alternative to the Midwinter Burning would go ahead. The children would bond in the shared enterprise, he announced. There was nothing like a play to bring people together. And a nativity? That would celebrate the birth of the Saviour, the Light of the World, and bring peace and goodwill to all.

Alfie glanced across the aisle to Mr Copper, who gave a sudden snort when the vicar announced his plan. Then the old man turned his head and his eyes met Alfie's. The words Mr Copper had murmured when Alfie had ridden into the village on Blossom echoed once more in Alfie's head. *Little lad, just like that one there. One who didn't belong. That's how it started, I tell you.*

Alfie still had no idea what Mr Copper had meant, but he felt a sliver of fear pierce his heart.

As the vicar moved on to practical matters regarding the nativity, Alfie's mind began to wander. He'd always hated nativity plays and never really known why. Now, somehow, it seemed all mixed up with the fate of the farm's pig. Baby Jesus had been born just so he could die later on the cross. How could you celebrate his birth knowing what horrible things were going to happen to him?

The vicar said that he would audition all the children – *all* of them, he stressed, looking directly at Alfie – in the middle of November. Rehearsals would then take place in the church every Monday after the evacuees' lessons had finished and before the village children's had begun.

"I'll make you a sandwich to take on Mondays," said Auntie Bell as she climbed into the cart after church. "Or you'll faint from hunger on the way home. I can make you a costume too. I wonder what part you'll play, birdie. Would you like to be one of the kings, maybe? Or a shepherd?"

DARKNESS RISING

Auntie Bell kept Alfie busy for the rest of Sunday, asking him to help her wash the yard down after milking and then muck out the pigsty. He had to give it a good scrub to get it ready for the next occupant, a piglet that would arrive in the spring.

Alfie didn't see Smidge all weekend. When he walked home from school on Monday, he hoped his friend would appear in the woods or somewhere along the river path but there was neither sight nor sound of him. Alfie lingered at the spot where the river narrowed, staring at the string of barbed wire, wondering when the fence and the sign telling trespassers they'd be prosecuted had been put back up. Still, Smidge didn't come. Nor was he by the deep pool. And he wasn't on the beach either, or anywhere on the zigzag path back through the woods to the farm.

"You're late," Auntie Bell told him when he finally gave up and went home. "Whatever kept you? I was starting to worry."

Alfie was bemused. He hadn't thought he'd stayed out any longer than he usually did. If anything, he'd walked home quicker without having Smidge to play with on the way. And yet more time than usual seemed to have passed.

It was the same the following day. And the one after that. A whole week went by in which Alfie didn't see Smidge once and he only just got back in time for lunch.

The days and nights crawled by. Anxiety began to gnaw at Alfie's insides. He was kicking himself for not having found out where Smidge lived because he had no idea where to look for him. Smidge had always just appeared, so Alfie never needed to think about it before. He should have found a way of asking, he thought. What kind of a friend was he? He should have asked about the other people too – the ones who'd been hunting that animal. Maybe they were Smidge's family, although he didn't really look like the rest of them. And the one in charge – the man who reminded Alfie of Billy Figgs' father – had clearly disliked Smidge. Had it been him who'd caused those bruises on his arm?

171

Another weekend passed and there was still no sign of Smidge. It wasn't until the next Wednesday afternoon – almost two weeks since he'd last seen his friend – that Alfie spotted Smidge when he was walking home from school.

Smidge was sitting on the large rock by the deep pool where the heron usually stood, so absorbed with whatever he was doing that he didn't look up.

Alfie was overwhelmed with relief. It felt like years since they'd seen each other. Everything would be all right now, he thought.

"Smidge!" he called, running over.

The boy started guiltily and, as he looked up, Alfie saw a shadow of fear cross his face. He was holding a knife in one hand, Alfie noticed, but he hid the other behind his back. When he saw it was Alfie, Smidge's shoulders relaxed a little.

As Alfie drew closer, he saw that Smidge's eyes were pink-rimmed as if he'd been crying.

"Are you all right?" asked Alfie, squatting down beside Smidge.

Smidge's left hand was still behind his back.

"What are you doing?" Alfie asked. "Can I see?"

He held out his palm and raised his eyebrows.

Smidge didn't look at all sure that he wanted to

show Alfie what he was doing. His face clouded for a moment and he chewed his lip while he stared at the ground. Then he seemed to make a decision. Smidge smiled weakly, brought his arm out from behind his back and put what he was holding into Alfie's hand.

It was the half-finished figure of a child with short, curling hair, carved from what looked like a piece of animal bone.

"Wow!" said Alfie. "Did you make this?"

"Smidge mek dis." He nodded nervously, as if fearing that Alfie would disapprove.

"It's amazing! You're incredible, Smidge!" The boy might not have understood the words, yet clearly understood that Alfie was impressed. He smiled properly now.

Taking the figure back, he showed Alfie what he was doing. The knife in his right hand was wooden-handled, but had the same chipped stone blade as the spearhead he'd given Alfie. He used it to shave little bits here and there off the bone, carving the rough, half-finished figure into a boy. A boy who wore shorts, and boots, and a coat. A boy who looked extraordinarily like Alfie.

Eyes round with wonder, Alfie whispered, "Is that me?"

Smidge nodded. "Effie... Un," he said, pointing

to Alfie first and then to the figure. "Effie... Oo... Un, oo Effies."

"Two Alfies! Brilliant!"

Both boys laughed. And then stopped as a shadow fell across them. Smidge's face was suddenly fearful.

Alfie spun around to see the man – the hunter who reminded him of Billy's father – looming so large he was blotting out the sky.

"Starver," said Smidge.

That must be his name, thought Alfie. Starver yelled something at Smidge and then stretched out his hand demanding to see what Smidge had carved. Reluctantly, the boy placed his precious carving on Starver's palm. When he examined it, Starver, for some inexplicable reason, seemed disgusted, regarding the beautifully carved figure as if it was a lump of rotting meat. Clutching it in his fist, he shouted more words at Smidge that made the boy flinch.

Still holding the carving in one hand, Starver seized Smidge's arm with the other, twisting it so hard the boy yelled out in pain. He began to push Smidge along the riverbank towards the beach.

Alfie, helpless and afraid, was frozen to the spot. Starver was a big, strong man and he was clearly angry. Alfie didn't have a hope of stopping him from hurting Smidge more.

Yet he couldn't just stand there! He had to do something.

He followed, stumbling after the pair, slipping in his haste, losing his footing on the mossy rock and scraping his leg painfully before falling into the water. By the time Alfie pulled himself out, the two figures had disappeared. And though Alfie followed at a run, he could neither catch up nor find any trace of them.

THE CHOSEN ONE

Auditions for the nativity play took place on Monday after morning lessons. Evacuees and village children stood in an awkward, uneasy line as they waited to be called up one by one to climb the steps to the pulpit and read a verse from the Bible as loudly as they could. It was a tiny church, but the pulpit steps were steep and some of the smaller ones could barely see over the lectern. The vicar stood at the back to assess their volume. When he'd listened to all the children, he allotted roles, beginning with the non-speaking parts. Violet's little brother was to be a sheep along with several similar-sized village children. Others were told they were going to be cows or chickens or camels. The shepherds and the three kings were named next. Carrie and Claire Thompson were to be part of the heavenly host. Billy Figgs was chosen to play King Herod. Violet Davies was the Virgin Mary.

Joe Copper was then called forward.

The vicar told him, "You will be Joseph. Hurry along. Go and stand next to Mary."

No couple had ever looked so miserable. It almost made Alfie laugh until the Reverend Braithwaite pointed at him, and then Alfie – who would really rather have avoided the whole thing – learned his fate.

"Alfie, isn't it? Alfie Wright? Well, Alfie, as you alone took no part in the disgraceful scenes we witnessed in the village the other week," the vicar declared, "it seems only fitting that you should play the part of the Angel Gabriel. You, my boy, are to be the divine messenger and bring word of peace and goodwill to all men."

"Hallelujah," muttered Billy Figgs and Joe Copper at exactly the same moment.

Auntie Bell was delighted by Alfie's news.

"I shall have to make you a very special costume!" she said. "A white tabard and a pair of wings. I can use real feathers. Do you proud, eh? It will give me something to do on these dark evenings. I shall kill a couple of the geese early. You'll look magnificent."

Alfie didn't much like the geese, which still chased

him every time he crossed the yard. Even so, it didn't seem right that a pair of them should die just so he could have their feathers as a costume for a play he didn't want to be in. His feelings must have shown on his face because she added, "They've all got to go soon, Alfie. I kill them in time for Christmas every year. People like a roast goose for their dinner; it's what I raise them for. They wouldn't be here at all otherwise."

Just like the pig, thought Alfie. And the baby Jesus. And the thousands and thousands of soldiers marching off to war. All being forced to sacrifice their lives so that people like him could live.

PLAYING WITH FIRE

The vicar's plan to bond the two warring groups of children worked. After a fashion. Evacuees and locals became firm friends during the very first rehearsal. But really, Alfie thought as he walked home afterwards, it wasn't the nativity play that had done it. What had cemented the children together was both sides finding a common enemy.

Him. He was It. Again.

Billy Figgs was to blame. Of course he was. But it was the vicar who had started it with all that talk of Alfie not being involved in the children's battle. He might not have meant to, but he'd made Alfie an object of hate and derision for both sides.

They had all been sitting down in the choir stalls at the front of the church for the rehearsal. Everyone with a speaking part had been given a script and Alfie had been reading out his lines, *Do not be afraid, Mary. You have found favour with God.*

Billy had whispered something to Violet and then elbowed her savagely in the ribs. She'd laughed – a tight, false-sounding giggle. Then Billy had said something to Joe Copper, who was sitting on the side closest to Alfie, and Alfie had heard the words clearly: "Bloody goody two shoes, ain't he?"

Joe had grinned and repeated, "Yes. Gabriel Goody Two Shoes, he is."

The whispering and giggling had spread through both evacuees and local children like scarlet fever until, magically, they were all united and Alfie Wright was Alfie Wrong once more. Gabriel Goody Two Shoes.

The vicar got so angry with his unruly cast he cut the first rehearsal short, sending the local children off to school and the evacuees back home.

Alfie walked slowly towards the farm along the valley path feeling more unhappy than he'd ever been. Before he'd met Smidge, he'd often been alone but never really felt lonely. He hadn't known what it was like to have a friend. He hadn't known you could laugh with someone until you felt so weak you could hardly stand. He hadn't known you could just sit quietly with the same person and watch the waves breaking on the shore.

He didn't know what was going on in Smidge's life, but felt deep down inside that something bad was happening to his friend. And now bad things were happening to Alfie again too and he had no idea what to do about any of it.

For a moment he toyed with the idea of telling Auntie Bell about Billy Figgs and Joe Copper. But he couldn't bear the idea of her looking at him the way his mother had the one time he'd told her about Billy's bullying: as if she was ashamed of his unpopularity, as if he'd done something to deserve it. His mother had said he had to fight his own battles and Auntie Bell was bound to say the same. And what could Auntie Bell do anyway? She couldn't be there all the time. There were a million and one ways that Billy could find to hurt him. And, now Billy had joined forces with Joe Copper, Alfie had no chance.

The second rehearsal the following Monday wasn't any better than the first. Billy Figgs and Joe Copper had become thick as thieves.

They were supposed to read through the script, that was all.

"I will show you all where to stand and when to

move later, after you have all learned your lines," the vicar said. "Which I expect you to have done by next week."

There was to be no giggling, he added sternly. No silliness. Lady Atherington was very keen for the nativity to be a success and he'd be having words with her if there was any more misbehaviour.

With the threat of Her Ladyship's displeasure hovering over them, the children sat in perfect silence for the rest of the rehearsal. There wasn't another whisper or a splutter from either Billy or Joe, but they hadn't stopped picking on Alfie. Instead of sniggering, they simply stared at him. And all the other children followed their lead for fear of what Billy and Joe would do to them if they stepped out of line.

Whenever it was Alfie's turn to speak, he could feel the great burden of attention crushing him to nothing. Two dozen pairs of eyes looking at him, scrutinizing him, weighing him up, finding him wanting. So Alfie stumbled over his lines. His tongue felt like a flannel in his mouth. He sweated hot and cold; his skin itched all over.

They inched slowly along, line by line, through the whole play and every second felt like torture.

At long, long last, the three kings arrived at the stable, handed over their gifts and, after Alfie had declared peace and goodwill to all men and led the heavenly host in a carol, it was over. For today, at any rate.

"Good effort, everyone," said the vicar. "Same time next week."

Without more ado the children spilled out of the choir stalls, an excited, giggling mass, pushing and shoving, chattering, filling the aisle so that Alfie couldn't get past them. He hung back, only leaving the church when the last child had gone out through the door.

Alfie was hoping to slip away quietly, but Billy Figgs and his new best friend Joe had stopped on the path for a chat. And whatever they were talking about was so interesting that all the other children had gathered to hear them.

Alfie was wondering if he could skirt around the crowd, but that would mean walking over the grass between the graves and he wasn't sure if that was allowed. Even if it was, it seemed disrespectful to the dead.

"What is this Darkness, then, Joe?" Billy asked loudly.

Alfie froze. He wanted to hear the answer.

"It's when bad things happen," said Joe with grim relish. "Terrible things."

183

"Like what?"

It was obvious that Joe didn't know. For a moment or two, his brow furrowed and he looked up at the sky as if hoping for inspiration.

"Blood gets spilled," he said at last. "There are murders and stabbings and suchlike. Grandpa's terrible worried. Tis only a month till Midwinter now. He says the Burning should happen, come what may, or else the whole village will get engulfed."

Billy looked thrilled at the prospect but Violet paled and Jack gave a soft whimper. Carrie and Claire took each other's hands and squeezed them tight.

The vicar, realizing that the children hadn't dispersed, had come to the church door and caught the tail end of Joe's grisly prediction.

"Children, children! Enough of this nonsense. It's superstition, that's all. Like throwing salt over your shoulder when you spill it."

"Keeps the devil away," muttered Joe.

"Goes in his eyes. Blinds 'im," agreed Billy.

Others were nodding as they all looked at the vicar.

"What rot!" said Reverend Braithwaite. "Really, you boys are old enough to know better." He'd clearly had enough of children for one day. With a dismissive wave of his hand, he turned away and disappeared back into the church, closing the door firmly behind him.

Billy returned to the topic of the Midwinter Burning.

"Is it just a bonfire though?" he asked. "Or is it like Guy Fawkes?"

"Oh yes, it's just like Guy Fawkes. We make ourselves a straw man – a scarecrow, if you like – to put on the bonfire. But, in the old days, it was even better than that." Joe Copper looked at Alfie, his eyes scalding Alfie's skin as he told Billy Figgs, "Grandpa says that way back – long, long ago – they didn't burn a straw man. They burned a real person. A little lad."

"A sacrifice, like?"

"That's right. A sacrifice."

"And how did they pick him?" asked Billy.

"They picked someone they didn't like. Someone who didn't belong."

Both boys looked at Alfie now. And Alfie didn't care any more about whether it was allowed or whether it was disrespectful to the dead. He ran over the grass, dodging between the graves, eyes boring into his back as he hurried out of the churchyard, jeering laughter echoing in his ears long after he was out of the village.

THE STONES

The morning after the rehearsal, Alfie woke up knowing that he simply couldn't face Billy or Joe or Violet or any of the other children that day. He just didn't have the strength. That particular Tuesday, he'd had enough.

It was almost exactly two weeks since he'd last seen Smidge. He'd been able to think of little else since then. Smidge was in his mind every waking moment and at night Alfie dreamed about him. He had no idea what to do. Should he look for him? Where? Should he tell someone? Who? He was sure that no one in the village had ever seen Smidge. Auntie Bell knew everything about everybody and she'd have mentioned the boy if she knew of his existence. For almost two weeks, he'd known deep down that there was no one to answer the questions that banged around inside his skull. He'd felt totally lost, not knowing what to do until that Tuesday morning, when the desire to avoid Billy and a determination to find Smidge collided in his head.

He wouldn't tell anyone what he was going to do. He'd let Auntie Bell think he was setting off for school. Instead, he'd go to the river. To the beach. To the spot where the kingfishers' nest was. He'd search all the places he'd ever been with Smidge. And if he couldn't find him? Well, then, he'd look for traces of him at least. Signs. Clues. He'd track Smidge down somehow; he had to.

He'd get told off for it later, he knew. You got in serious trouble for playing truant. Auntie Bell would be upset and the idea of letting her down when she'd always been so very kind to him filled Alfie with guilt. But he'd go mad if he didn't do *something*.

When he left the farm, Alfie was planning to go to the beach. He'd start there, he thought, and then work his way upriver towards the village. The sky was grey as lead and it was drizzling, so he turned up his collar to stop the water dripping down his neck.

As he reached the place where the paths divided, the pull towards the stones was stronger than ever. It wasn't a tug under the ribs this time. It was a steady heave, as if the invisible string had grown into a rope and there was someone at the other end reeling him in. There was no resisting the strength of it. Alfie obeyed, and turned towards the headland.

The first time he'd stood on the headland looking at the stones, he'd thought they were waiting for something. Someone. There had been a vague sense of anticipation. What was vague then had grown much stronger now. All the way there, the air had been thick with it, shimmering, like the heat off a London street in the middle of summer. He walked along the cliff path and down into the wooded valley. He crossed the bridge without even glancing at the waterfall and started up the other side, not pausing for breath as he had done the first time he'd walked this way. Though the path was as steep and a familiar stitch had begun to stab at his side, he didn't pause to catch his breath. The stones wanted him to keep moving. As he climbed, the soft, steady drizzle stopped as suddenly as if a tap had been turned off. The temperature plummeted and the air became so cold and crisp, Alfie's breath billowed into clouds. When he emerged from the woods onto the headland, he saw the grass and heather was silvered with frost.

He walked slowly towards the stones, standing strong and silent, outlined against a clear blue sky. He felt them tugging him towards the centre of the ring, yet, in the same way that he hadn't wanted to walk over the graves in the churchyard, he didn't want to set foot inside the circle either. It would be like trespass. No ... worse than that. It would be desecration. There was a sacred, powerful magic to the place, Alfie thought as he drew closer. And a sense of gathering darkness. The feeling that something bad was about to happen was crushing. Overwhelming.

He didn't want to be overwhelmed!

He didn't want to be crushed!

He forced himself to stop. He planted his feet firmly in the frostbitten heather.

The vicar's words ran through his head and he repeated them out loud: "It's superstition, that's all."

Silly superstition.

Alfie tried to get a grip of himself. He was meant to be looking for Smidge, for heaven's sake! And there was no sign of his friend up here. He turned full circle, looking inland to see if he could spot the farm and the road to the village, but they were hidden by trees – or else he was looking in the wrong direction again. He could see the beach clearly enough, though. That was where he really wanted to go. So why couldn't he drag himself away? Were the stones keeping him here? But that was a silly idea! Stones didn't have any power!

"Stupid Alfie," he said aloud. "You're being stupid. They're lumps of rock, that's all." He needed to find Smidge. He had to go and look for clues so he could track him down. But, once more, he couldn't seem to tug his eyes from the stone circle.

"You're just lumps of rock," he told them. "You look like grown-ups gossiping after church. Or little kids, playing ring-a-ring o' roses." He lowered his voice and told himself, "There's nothing to be scared of."

Trying to calm his loudly thumping heart, he hummed the tune of "Ring-a-Ring o' Roses" and then started singing the words aloud. The frost on the heather and grass glinted like diamonds. It was beautiful, but the sight didn't calm him. Heart still thudding, he sang the words once more, at the top of his voice. When he got to the end, he heard someone calling his name.

"Effie!"

And, suddenly, there was Smidge, stepping out of the shadow of the trees, running towards Alfie, a smile on his face.

A great wave of relief washed over Alfie. It was so strong it dizzied him and he had to put a hand on the nearest stone to steady himself.

"Where have you been?" he said, as Smidge reached him.

Smidge raised his hand in the usual greeting but, instead of slapping palms, Alfie seized Smidge's hand in both of his, scared he might disappear again.

"Are you all right? Why haven't I seen you for so long? What have you been doing? Has that man been hurting you? I was worried!"

Smidge was unable to follow the stream of questions so Alfie simplified things.

"Smidge happy?" he asked, putting on a bright smile. "Smidge sad?" Alfie turned his mouth down and, with his fingers, traced lines of imaginary tears running down his face.

The boy responded by saying his own name, "Smidge," pointing two fingers to his own eyes, and then, pointing to Alfie's, "Effie." Then he grinned broadly.

Alfie took that to mean that Smidge was happy now he'd seen Alfie.

"Me too," he said, copying the gestures. "Alfie see Smidge. Alfie happy."

Alfie wanted to find a way of asking where Smidge lived, and what was happening to him. Who was the man? Was he in trouble? His mind raced wondering how to do it. Before Alfie could say anything, Smidge started humming the tune of "Ring-a-Ring o' Roses" that Alfie had been singing.

Smidge wasn't getting it quite right, so Alfie hummed it for him. Smidge copied the tune until he got it straight.

Alfie started teaching him the song, getting him to repeat the words until they were clear. And singing in the cold, crisp air in the bright sunshine filled them both with a kind of excited happiness.

"There's a dance, too. Like this."

Alfie grabbed Smidge's hands and took a step sideways. Smidge grasped the concept immediately and, before long, they were both skipping and dancing to the rhyme. They spun around, singing their hearts out.

When they came to the "all fall down" bit, Alfie hurled himself onto the ground and lay on his back, staring up at the sky. Smidge did the same.

Soon they were back up again and wheeling in such tight circles they made themselves giddy. Heads reeling, without realizing it, they moved from the outer edge of the stones into the circle. They twirled until they were so dizzied they both fell over onto the frosted grass.

And then they heard a yell of outrage.

The stones themselves seemed appalled, standing

stiff-backed and furious. But the yell was Starver's. The man was there at the edge of the circle, looking in, white-faced with rage. Beside him stood an old woman. An ancient, stooped figure who should have looked frail but instead exuded power. She wore a cloak of furs, a necklace of what looked like beads and animal teeth. Feathers were braided into her thinning hair.

Her face! That expression! It wasn't just a normal grown-up's irritation. Alfie and Smidge hadn't been a bit too loud, or a little bit naughty. The rage etched into every line of her wrinkled skin told Alfie they'd done something terribly, terribly wrong. It was like being caught dancing on gravestones or spitting in the communion wine. They hadn't just been had; they'd been sinful.

Smidge was deathly pale, whispering words that Alfie couldn't understand, but it was clear that he was apologizing.

The old woman came towards them, stepping into the circle and meeting them at its heart, although Starver still lingered outside. She put a hand on Smidge's shoulder. Bony fingers, digging into the boy's flesh, steering him away from Alfie.

"Sorry!" Alfie said, following them. "It was all my fault. I started it."

There was no reply. The old woman didn't even turn her head to look at him. She ignored Alfie as if he simply didn't exist.

The moment Smidge was outside the circle of stones, Starver was before him, his hand raised as if he was about to strike the boy. The old woman was saying something. Barking words out like bullets. She seemed to be giving orders. Commanding Starver not to hurt Smidge? Or telling him he should? Alfie didn't wait to find out.

He'd never been much good at fighting his own battles, but he could fight Smidge's.

Half the size and strength of Starver, Alfie didn't stop to think. He swung blindly at the man with both fists.

And the strangest of all the strange things that Alfie had experienced since coming to Coombe Farm occurred. His fists passed through Starver's flesh as if he wasn't there.

GHOSTS

For a moment, Alfie and Smidge looked at each other, bewildered. And then the scene changed as suddenly as if a light switch had been flicked.

Drizzle falling steadily from a leaden grey sky was blown by the wind across the sea. In the distance, black storm clouds billowed on the horizon. There was no frost. No golden sunlight.

And the stones! What had happened to the stones? Their edges looked rounded, as if they had been smoothed by centuries of wind and rain. They were sloping at odd angles and covered in the same moss and lichen that grew on the trough at Coombe Farm where the churns were set to cool after milking. One of them had completely fallen over and was lying on its back in the long grass. Two others were leaning drunkenly together, supporting each other like men emerging from a pub. Inland, Alfie could see smoke rising through the chimney of Coombe Farm. There was the winding lane that led to the village.

But Smidge, Starver and the old woman had completely disappeared. Alfie was alone.

"Smidge!" he yelled. "Smidge! Smidge!"

He called his friend's name until his throat was dry.

"Smidge! Come back! Please, come back!"

The boy didn't reappear.

And, deep in his belly, Alfie knew that he wouldn't.

All the uneasy feelings Alfie had pushed from his mind these past few weeks came flooding into his head. He knew without doubt that Smidge was as real as he was. But Alfie also knew that he shouldn't have seen him. They didn't belong in the same world. Smidge was from a different time altogether. A time when people hunted with spears and wore clothes stitched together from animal hides. The clues had always been there, but he'd not wanted to see them. The way the weather changed and the seasons slipped when Smidge appeared, the way the carpet of blue flowers came and went, even the barbed wire and the sign about trespassers... Being with Smidge had been so wonderful, he hadn't wanted to think about what any of that might mean. Now the knowledge was inescapable. Alfie had seen someone he wasn't meant to. Made friends with someone he shouldn't ever have met.

The worst thing of all was that he suspected he'd got Smidge into terrible, terrible trouble. He'd seen the look on the old woman's face. And she seemed to be someone very important. What's more, she'd stepped into the heart of the circle while Starver had hovered at the edge as if he didn't dare to. And if Starver was scared to set foot in there, then Smidge most definitely shouldn't have.

How must it have looked to the old woman and to Starver? Smidge singing a strange song whose words made no sense to them, dancing and spinning around in a sacred place with a friend who was invisible to their eyes? For a long time, Alfie sat in the sodden heather, shaking with misery, turning things over and over in his fear-numbed mind.

Was Starver a ghost?

Was Smidge?

No! Ghosts couldn't catch fish and roast them over a fire or burn pictures into driftwood. They couldn't swap spearheads for magnifying glasses with their friends. Could they? Surely not? And yet what other explanation could there be?

*   *   *

197

While Alfie was sitting in the heather the wind grew steadily stronger and the drizzle turned to heavy rain. At last he got to his feet.

The walk back to the farm was slippery and muddy and miserable. The steep path streamed with rainwater and a few times Alfie lost his footing altogether and went skidding downhill, crashing into trees, scratching his arms on brambles.

He had lost all track of time by now, but, by chance, he arrived at Coombe Farm just as Auntie Bell was setting the table for lunch.

"Oh my goodness!" she said when she saw Alfie coming through the door, caked in mud and soaked to the skin. "I thought you must be having a terrible walk home from school, but I never imagined it would be that bad! You're filthy! Why ever didn't you stick to the lanes? Go straight upstairs and put on some clean, dry things before you catch your death."

She didn't know he'd played truant then. Word hadn't reached her yet. He supposed she'd find out on Sunday after church. He ought to be worried, but school and everyone in it seemed unimportant now.

Alfie got changed and dried his hair with a towel as best he could. He desperately needed to talk to someone. Something was dreadfully wrong. But there was no one he could go to other than Auntie Bell. She would probably give him the Mr Moore look again, but he had to risk it.

The wind's strength increased throughout the afternoon.

"Tis blowing itself up into a proper storm, Alfie dear," said Auntie Bell shortly after lunch. "A gale like this causes no end of damage. We'd best make ready. Get the birds in early, I reckon, so they don't get blown clean away."

Looking after the poultry had become Alfie's job, so he set off across the yard with his pouch of corn. The hens were obliging enough, following him into the small barn when he filled the feeders, but the geese were stubborn and argumentative, indignantly refusing to be shut in early.

"I'm just trying to keep you safe!" he told them.

The stupid things were having none of it and the harder he tried, the more they refused to cooperate. And either they'd got more cunning, or he was being slow and stupid with the walking stick, because, once or twice, they managed to nip his calves and leave half-moon shaped bruises in his flesh. In the end, Ted had to get Jake and Sam to herd them in.

Afternoon milking was done in the howling wind. Alfie strained the full buckets of milk into churns with clumsy, cold hands as the driving rain found its way past his collar and trickled down his neck and chest. When they at last herded the cows back to their field, Alfie got so thoroughly soaked that he needed yet another change of clothes.

It wasn't until suppertime that Alfie had a chance to talk to Auntie Bell.

He had no idea where to begin. So many thoughts whirled around his head, he couldn't catch them and put them into the right words. In the end he simply asked, "Have you ever seen a ghost?"

Across the table, Ted stopped chewing and stared at Alfie.

Auntie Bell laughed.

"No!" she said. "Someone been filling your head with tales, have they? Tis all that silly talk of the Burning, I expect. Mr Copper has got such a bee in his bonnet about it all he's turning everyone's minds inside out. Pay it no heed. There's no such things as ghosts, Alfie dear. They're stories to frighten children with, that's all. Don't you go paying any attention. When a body dies, the soul moves on. To heaven, if you've lived a good life and said your prayers. Or to the other place, if you haven't. Either way, it's for the good Lord to decide."

And then – very deliberately, Alfie thought – Auntie

Bell changed the subject. She asked Ted if he thought Primrose was perhaps a little lame, and was Buttercup's left eye looking weepy as though it might have been scratched? She talked without seeming to pause to eat or breathe but soon enough her plate was cleared and she got up to fetch pudding from the pantry.

When Alfie and Ted were alone, Ted leaned forward and suddenly said more to Alfie than he'd ever done before.

"I seen something. Almost. When I was your age, I used to think I was being watched. Thought if I could only turn my head quick enough, I'd catch whoever it was. But I never did."

Alfie remembered the conversation he'd had with Auntie Bell when he'd first seen the hunters in the wood.

"Auntie said you went looking for elves and pixies when you were small."

"No! I was never after those, no matter what Mother thought! Look here, lad, I don't say ghosts exist," he continued quickly. "But I don't say they don't neither. There are some places around here that feel haunted, I reckon, by the old ones."

"The old ones?"

"The people who were here before the village

was built. The ones who hauled those stones up the cliffs and stood them there. What for? I wonder. Some powerful belief must have made them do that. And there those stones stand still, all these years later. The old ones were born, died, buried here. Tis bound to leave an impression. We forget the ancient ways but the land doesn't. They sink into the very earth and the rocks beneath. Sometimes, if you're listening, you can catch an echo."

"But why would a ghost walk the Earth?"

"Ah, well, there's a question. What makes a ghost a ghost? I wonder. Why does a soul linger on Earth? Is it because something went wrong? Something so bad that it jars against Mother Nature herself?"

Alfie opened his mouth. He wanted to say that something bad was happening right now to his friend Smidge. *Was* it happening now, though? Or had it already happened? He suddenly wanted to tell Ted everything. But then Auntie Bell came back with the apple crumble and Ted got up to check on the animals and the conversation was over.

PART IIII

The Seer's heart was heavy. Her vision, that she had once thought so clear, was clouded. Time and time again, the Goddess had put Smidge into her head when she had been thinking of Midwinter and, time and time again, she had ignored it. The Seer's own thoughts and feelings had blinded her to the wishes of the Goddess. She had grown too fond of Smidge these last few moons to see him for what he truly was.

The situation grieved her almost beyond bearing. The strange-looking dreamer had been so happy of late. Though the hunters shunned his company and he spent all his time alone, he had not seemed lonely. Indeed, he had looked more content than she had ever known him.

He had begun to create extraordinary things, burning images into wood using a strange, transparent disc of rock. A disc of rock whose source he could not or would not explain. And then Starver had seen him using his knife to make a peculiar human figure from bone. The Seer had taken it as a sign that Smidge was exceptional. A visionary. A child who might one day become a seer, like herself. Indeed, a child that may conceivably grow up to lead the clan, if only they would let him.

Starver had disagreed. Smidge was performing bad magic by creating such images, Starver said. It was witchcraft. And it was true that no one in the clan had ever done such things. It unnerved them.

Starver had always believed the boy to be sent by a demon and she had always resisted the idea.

But now the Seer had seen Smidge, with her own eyes, desecrating the sacred heart of the stone circle. Despoiling it. Dancing wildly, screaming aloud words that no human could understand, as if possessed by all the dark demons of the underworld.

STORMY WEATHER

By the time Alfie went to bed that night, the storm was raging. The wind howled around the house like a wild animal and rain came in sheets, wave after wave lashing the farmhouse. Hail rattled down the chimney. He didn't think he'd sleep at all, but, around midnight, he fell into uneasy dreams. Images unravelled across his eyelids like spools of film.

Smidge, Starver and the old woman were tangled up together with Joe Copper and Billy Figgs and the vicar. The nativity play. Midwinter Burning. Past. Present. Future. All overlapping. All mixed together.

Things had gone wrong for Smidge and it was Alfie's fault. Alfie had caused it all.

He dreamed he was in the kitchen, arguing with Auntie Bell.

"The Burning is evil," he said.

"Nonsense," she replied. "'Tis an old tradition. Just a piece of silliness."

"It isn't! It isn't!" he cried. "It must have started somewhere. Like with Guy Fawkes and Bonfire Night. Guy Fawkes was a real person once, wasn't he?"

Alfie knew in his heart that the Midwinter Burning had started with a real person. Mr Copper wasn't making up stories to scare children; he was telling the truth. The old ones had hurt someone. Killed them. Someone innocent, who shouldn't have died. What the old ones did was terribly wrong. So terribly wrong it had echoed down the centuries. Wrongness had seeped like poison into the earth and the rocks beneath. Their crime had jarred against Mother Nature herself.

He tried to speak, but no words came out. And Auntie Bell was looking at him the way people looked at old Mr Moore. And then, suddenly, his mother was in the kitchen too, in her dancing shoes and her blood-red lipstick, saying to Auntie Bell, "Alfie should be locked up. I always knew it. Put him in the loony bin where he belongs."

Now Alfie was up at the stones, standing beside the old woman, watching Smidge whirling around, singing and laughing completely on his own, looking like a lunatic.

And then the landscape changed again and Alfie found himself in the village square where a torchlit procession was taking place. The faces of Auntie Bell, Ted, Miss Bottomley, the vicar, Mr Copper and Joe, all dressed in furs, carrying spears, distorted in the flames, melting, blurring, turning into the faces of Smidge's people. He and Smidge were surrounded. And then they were pushed forward. Along the ghost road, over the fields, straight to the headland. And the stones were standing upright, free of moss and lichen, sharp-edged, unsoftened by wind and weather. A bonfire. A raised axe.

Alfie screamed and jerked awake. But the screaming continued. And it wasn't coming from him. The rain had stopped though the wind still howled. And there was another sound too, above and beyond it. A wailing, followed by low sobbing.

Smidge! He was there somewhere, weeping his heart out, Alfie was sure of it.

He leapt from his bed and ran down the dark steps into the kitchen. Tearing open the door, he ran barefoot out into the night.

Alarmed, the geese in the barn started hissing and the dogs barked. Alfie screamed over them, "Where are you, Smidge? Where are you? I'm coming!"

From somewhere close, he heard a tremendous

ripping noise and then a terrible thud as if something very large had toppled over. Then the weeping came again.

"Smidge! SMIDGE!"

Alfie's screams woke Auntie Bell and Ted, who came downstairs – pulling on wellingtons, buttoning coats over their nightclothes – and out into the yard, looking pale and dazed with sleep, buffeted by the wind. Ted had a rifle in his hand.

"Whatever's the matter, Alfie?" asked Auntie Bell.

Before Alfie could reply, there was a distant rumble from the direction of the cliffs, then an almighty crash that Alfie could feel through his feet, as though the land itself was trembling in pain. The three of them peered into the darkness, eyes straining towards the headland.

"What on earth was that?" asked Auntie Bell.

Ted shook his head. "No idea. Plane come down, maybe?"

But there were no flames, no plumes of smoke.

Yet something dreadful had happened. Something had torn, ripped apart, Alfie could feel it. He shivered.

"Come back inside," Auntie Bell said. She reached and took Alfie's hand, gently tugging him towards her.

Alfie tried to pull away. But then Ted put his big, farmer's palm on Alfie's shoulder and said, "Can't do nothing about anything while it's dark, lad."

Alfie allowed himself to be steered back into the house, where Auntie Bell made hot milk and honey, holding the cup to Alfie's lips as if he was a baby.

After that, they all returned to their beds. It was a long time before Alfie slept. When he did, he dreamed of Smidge, alone in the dark, hunched into a ball, afraid, crying. Not for what had happened in the past.

For what was yet to come.

VICTIM

By the next morning, the storm had blown itself out. Alfie woke to the sounds of Auntie Bell stoking up the range and putting the kettle on. Outside, everything was still. When he finally opened the blackout shutters, the sun poured in, dazzling him. Out in the yard, the rain had washed everything clean. The birds were singing their hearts out. The world looked bright and new made.

And it shouldn't! Everything felt wrong, so everything should have looked wrong too. Instead of lifting his heart, the view out of the window angered Alfie. He felt betrayed.

His fingers were slow and stiff as he dressed, his limbs heavy, as if they'd been filled with sand.

A tree had come down near the front of the house,

Auntie Bell told him when he descended the steps to the kitchen.

"No damage done, mind. We had a lucky escape. Ted will get Frankie to come and help chop the thing up. We shall have plenty of firewood from it, so tis a blessing in a manner of speaking."

Auntie Bell said it was the tree falling that made the noise.

Alfie knew she was wrong. The falling tree must have made the ripping sound and then the thud, but that had happened before Auntie Bell and Ted came out into the yard. The sound afterwards came from the headland. Something had happened up there. He had to know what it was.

And so, after milking, instead of going to school, Alfie slipped away once more to the stones.

This time there was no tug where the paths divided. Nothing drew him across the field, along the cliff path and down into the wooded valley. Nothing urged him to hurry, to move faster. He hadn't realized quite how strong the pulling sensation had been until it stopped. It was strange. He almost wished he could feel it now. Or, if not, the opposite: that the stones were forcing him away. Now they weren't doing anything. It wasn't that they didn't want him up there any more. They just didn't care. He was unimportant. He had no idea what he should or shouldn't have done or when or why or how. Yet he felt completely sure that he'd had his chance and messed it up. He was too late.

That sense of terrible failure grew and grew until it was so heavy he felt like a rock was pressing down on his shoulders. The path was slippery. He took three steps forward and slipped back one. It took an age to reach the place where the trees thinned and he could look out onto the open headland.

When he did, he could scarcely believe what he saw. All the breath in his lungs was sucked out of him. He gasped and clutched his chest.

Auntie Bell had warned him about not climbing the cliffs. She'd told him on that first day, when she'd sent him off exploring on his own, that they sometimes crumbled.

He hadn't really known what she'd meant. He'd imagined that maybe a rock or two sometimes came loose and slid into the sea. He'd never dreamed of anything like this.

There had been a landslide.

Half the headland had collapsed. It had simply gone, as if a bomb had been dropped on it. Solid rock had cracked apart and slid into the sea, taking half the stone circle with it.

214

What was now the land's edge looked as though it had been severed with a giant knife.

Without conscious thought, with only a numb horror filling his brain, Alfie's feet propelled him towards the cliff edge. The headland was ripped through, exposing what lay beneath the grass and heather. Grey rock. Black earth.

And, deep in the black earth, something... Alfie collapsed onto the ground and heaved up his breakfast.

He looked again, unable to believe what he could see and yet, at the same time, feeling he'd always known what was there.

Standing out, ghastly pale against the dark soil ... bones.

A skeleton with its hand clearly visible, stick-thin fingers raised as if in greeting.

BLOOD SACRIFICE

Alfie didn't know how long he knelt on the newly torn cliff edge, unable to move, unable to tear his eyes away from the skeletal hand.

He didn't remember getting back to the farmhouse.

For days, he was confined to his bed. He was hot and cold all over and so weak he could barely stand. Auntie Bell thought he'd caught a chill and that he was delirious with fever, but it was grief and guilt that made his head pound and his body shake. Over and over again, he mumbled, "Smidge! Sorry, Smidge! All my fault. My fault. Mine."

The police must have come. They must have examined the bones and decided they were old. They must have called in experts, because suddenly there were two archaeologists staying in the house. There was no hotel in the village and Coombe Farm was not only nearer to the stones, but Auntie Bell had spare rooms to offer Professor Shaw and Professor Higgins. Alfie could hear their voices drifting up from the kitchen sometimes. Posh old men, who spoke to each other in clipped, BBC-announcer sort of voices, using words so long that Alfie couldn't understand most of them. They were conducting a thorough investigation of the burial site, according to Auntie Bell. They'd assured her that the bones were ancient. The skeleton belonged to someone who'd died thousands of years ago. She spoke as if that should be some sort of comfort, but Alfie cried harder than ever.

"How did he die? How did he die?"

"A blow to the back of the head, they say. It must have happened quick. Can't have suffered hardly at all."

"Why? Why was he killed?"

Auntie Bell hesitated and a shadow passed over her face. "Professor Shaw and Professor Higgins think maybe it was a sacrifice," she said. And then she went on quickly, "But I'm sure it can't have been anything as nasty as that. I reckon it was an accident, maybe when they were first building that stone circle. Poor little lad. He can't have been any older than you."

MOURNING

More days passed. Professor Shaw and Professor Higgins had been gone for some time before Alfie was well enough to go out of doors again. When he did, he found the wind on his face and the weak winter sunshine soothed him a little. The routine of the farm was calming, the company of the animals comforting. Most of the geese had already been killed for Christmas and the ones left were too shocked to try pecking him. Jake and Sam, the dogs Alfie wasn't supposed to make a fuss of, would sit with him, leaning against his legs while he ate his supper, or resting their heads in his lap. And even though they were working dogs and it might spoil them, Ted turned a blind eye.

The discovery of a boy's body, the landslide and the loss of half the stones had shaken the village to its core. Everyone agreed that it meant something, but no one could agree what.

On the second Sunday in December, Auntie Bell decided that Alfie was well enough to accompany her and Ted to church.

"It will do you good, birdie," she said. "Get things back to normal, like."

And yet she and Ted stuck tightly either side of Alfie like bodyguards, escorting him into church so quickly and efficiently that no one had a chance to talk to him.

It didn't stop them looking though. Violet gazed at him for almost the whole length of the service. Joe's and Billy's eyes kept darting gleefully at the boy who had discovered the bones.

Even the vicar stared as Alfie arrived. When it was time for his sermon, the vicar pushed aside the sheaf of notes he usually read from. Instead, he launched into a long and rambling speech about the need to put the past and its heathen practices behind them. He told the congregation solemnly that the good Lord abhorred such things. The hand of God had destroyed the pagan circle, he said: there could be no doubt of that.

Afterwards, Auntie Bell and Ted hustled Alfie out

of church and through the graveyard as quickly as they could. As they climbed back up onto the cart, he could hear Mr Copper saying loudly to his grandson, "The vicar's a fool. There's none so blind as them that won't see. That there landslide was a warning, plain as day. A sign of things to come. If we don't have the Burning, the Darkness will be on us, swallowing everything."

On Monday Alfie had to go back to school and Auntie Bell and Ted couldn't protect him there. Before he left Coombe Farm, he wrapped up Smidge's spearhead in a handkerchief and stowed it in his pocket as a kind of talisman.

It did nothing to defend him from the other children. They had buzzed for two weeks with talk of the stones and the body that had been buried there. And, now the boy at the centre of it all was amongst them once more, fuel was thrown on the fire. They crowded around him at playtime, eyes wide with ghoulish delight.

Alfie was the centre of attention. The star of the show. The hero. And maybe if he'd been a different boy he would have stepped up and satisfied their appetite. Maybe he could have finally made friends with Billy and the rest of them. He could have been Alfie Right.

But he was Alfie Wrong. And there was no changing that. Thinking – no ... *knowing* – that it was Smidge who had been killed and buried there left a sadness so deep that Alfie couldn't say a word. The more his classmates pressed him, the more he clammed up. Then, finally, he burst into tears.

And big boys weren't supposed to cry.

"Bonkers," was Billy Figgs' damning verdict. "He's off his rocker. Like old Mr Moore. Best keep away from him, eh? Might be catching."

After school that Monday, there was the horror of the nativity play rehearsal to endure. They'd got behind because of Alfie's illness. It was only ten days until the performance now, and the vicar was in a flap. Determined that it should be a success, he'd scheduled extra rehearsals for Wednesday and Friday.

While Alfie had been ill, Auntie Bell had made his costume. A worn pair of Ted's sandals kept from when he was a boy. A white tabard made out of an old bedsheet that was so large he could drape it over his normal clothes. A pair of wings so lifelike that he felt he could almost take flight and soar away. They seemed like the only real and substantial things in the church – everything else felt like a dream.

Between scenes, Joe Copper was still talking

about the Midwinter Burning, full of his Grandpa's threats and warnings.

"Mother Nature is angry," he told Violet as they waited for the shepherds and their unruly sheep to join them at the crib. "If the Midwinter Burning don't go ahead, something terrible will happen."

"Like what?" asked Violet.

"Hitler will invade. We shall lose the war. Something like that. Grandpa says Mother Earth doesn't want no straw man. Blood should be shed, he says. The way it was in the olden days."

Alfie left as soon as he could, half running down the aisle and out of the church the moment the rehearsal was over. He paid no heed to the footsteps behind him until he reached the edge of the village.

"Are you all right?"

Someone had followed him. And when he stopped to see who it was, Violet dodged around him and stood in his way.

She looked at him, head on one side.

Alfie tried to sidestep her but she put her hands on her hips, making herself look so big he took a step back. At least she was alone, that was something to be grateful for.

"Are you all right?" she said again gently, and she looked as if she minded about the answer.

But Alfie felt cross and tired. He didn't want to talk to Violet; he wanted to see Smidge!

"Get out of my way," he growled. And when she didn't, he pushed past her.

Violet called after him, "I'm just trying to be friendly!"

Alfie didn't answer. He didn't want another friend. Having friends hurt.

COMFORT AND JOY

At last the day came. The twenty-first of December. Midwinter. The villagers would usually be building a bonfire, forming a procession, burning a straw man. At night, they'd drive out the darkness and at dawn welcome the rising sun and the turning of the year.

But now Europe was at war. Soldiers were being sacrificed, not straw men. This year, there was only the nativity play. A happy celebration of a baby, destined to be nailed to a cross. A baby, doomed to die for everybody else's sins.

Alfie felt hollowed out. The world looked the same, sounded the same, but nothing felt right. It had all been poisoned by the dreadful wrongness of what had happened to Smidge. On top of that horror was the ache of missing him, of having made a friend only to lose him. Alfie was almost crippled with pain.

The performance for parents and host families was to take place in the afternoon. School finished early that morning so the children could have a final dress rehearsal.

It was a comfortless, joyless affair. The children were sulky and bored. The donkey – loaned by Lady Atherington for the occasion – was a bad tempered, stubborn thing that deposited a huge pile of dung in the church aisle and then refused to carry Mary a step further. Violet – who seemed terrified of the creature – slithered off its back in such haste she dropped the baby Jesus doll on his head and cracked his china skull.

Alfie stood, staring at the broken infant while the vicar arranged for the donkey to be taken back to the Manor in disgrace. After that, he gave his cast a stern talking-to.

"Hope," said the vicar. "The nativity story is all about hope. Redemption. The birth of a child who brings light to the world and salvation for us all."

"Salvation".

The word lit a flame in Alfie's head as he stood, only half listening to the rest of the vicar's words.

Smidge was some sort of ghost. What had Ted said? Ghosts walked the Earth because something had gone wrong. And it had gone terribly, terribly wrong. Alfie had unwittingly seen to that.

The flame in Alfie's head flickered and then grew stronger.

A whisper of a thought ran through his mind. A question.

Suppose that what had gone wrong could be put right?

ANGELS AND DEMONS

The performance of the nativity play was torture. Alfie's tongue seemed to have turned into wood. He could barely get his lines out and at one point he forgot them altogether.

Reverend Braithwaite had to hiss at him from the sidelines, "He shall bring peace on Earth!"

The vicar repeated it twice before Alfie even noticed. His mind was too busy, spinning with ideas. He was going to save Smidge. He had to. How? Where? What should he do?

While Joseph and Mary asked if there was room at the inn, Alfie slipped his hands into the pockets of the shorts he was wearing under his bedsheet tabard. His fingers closed around Smidge's spearhead, still wrapped in the handkerchief.

As the play went on, a plan began to form, shadowy at first but then more substantial.

Alfie knew that old people eventually died. If they were lucky, they fell asleep in their beds and didn't wake up. If they were unlucky, they got sick and died in hospital. Or they had accidents like getting run over by a bus or something. Whatever happened, they were usually buried in a different place from the one where they'd died.

Except Smidge hadn't just died, he'd been killed. Alfie could hardly bear to think about it but he had to. The professors said he'd been sacrificed. It must have been some sort of ritual and the stones – as far as he could see – were like an ancient church or cathedral or something. It seemed likely that Smidge had been killed and buried in the same place. Somehow, his death had started the whole village tradition of the Midwinter Burning. Alfie had to intervene tonight, he was sure of it.

He'd have to give Auntie Bell and Ted the slip. He glanced out of the church window. It was about an hour until sunset, he thought. Maybe a bit longer. As soon as the play was over – if he was lucky, if he really hurried all the way – he should be able to get to the stones just before it. And after that? He'd have to wait and see, he supposed. He'd stay there until sunrise if he had to! The play seemed to drag on for ever. Each second seemed to last a minute, each minute an hour.

Eventually the baby Jesus was laid in the manger but the shepherds took an age to arrive. As for the three kings...

"Hurry up!" Alfie wanted to shout at them. "We haven't got all day! Get moving!"

They edged up the aisle, inch by inch, agonizingly slowly.

As soon as they had handed over their gifts, Alfie shot up the stepladder and stood, arms outstretched, flanked by the angels of the heavenly host overlooking the crib while the rest of the cast knelt in homage to the infant Saviour. He declared peace on Earth and goodwill to all men, they sang "Away in a Manger" and at last it was over. Once the applause had died down Mary was helped on to the donkey with the Baby Jesus, and Joseph led it down the aisle. The rest of the children followed, past Lady Atherington's growling dogs. After that they were all supposed to go over to the schoolroom, and squeeze in to change into their normal, everyday clothes.

All except Alfie.

Once he'd scrambled down from the ladder, there was no time to waste. He hurried out of the churchyard, straight past the schoolroom door and headed out of the village.

But he'd reckoned without Billy Figgs and Joe Copper, who noticed Alfie darting away, still in his wings and tabard. Both boys stepped back out into the road.

"Where are you going?" called Joe.

"Nowhere," said Alfie over his shoulder.

"You're going nowhere in a terrible hurry, ain't you?" Billy shouted. "What are you up to?"

Alfie didn't answer. He had to keep moving.

The two boys looked at each other. Billy gave Joe a mean little grin.

"Let's follow him!"

Alfie quickened his pace. Someone – it might have been Violet – yelled "No!" and, "Leave him alone, you big bullies!"

It didn't make any difference; Billy and Joe were coming after him, so Alfie started to run. Behind him he could hear the boys' feet, pounding on the hard road.

Perhaps it started as a game. In just a few heartbeats, it became a chase.

"Get him!" Billy roared.

And, suddenly, their blood was up. Excitement flooded through their veins. Billy and Joe were hunters now. Alfie was their prey.

Alfie realized that this was it. The Darkness wasn't coming. It was here. It wasn't a force that came from outside. It came from within. Hate that poisoned minds and hearts and souls, uniting people when they found a victim. Someone different. Someone who didn't quite fit in. Someone to blame when things went wrong.

If Billy and Joe caught up with him, they would hurt him; Alfie was in no doubt about that. Yet he knew where he was going and they didn't. For now, at least, he had a small advantage.

He'd reached the place where the lane divided. The left fork led towards Coombe Farm, the right to Atherington Manor. The most direct route to the stones.

Crossing Her Ladyship's land was forbidden, Alfie knew that and Joe Copper must know it too. But Lady Atherington was still at the church. Her dogs were still tied up in the village. If Alfie took the right-hand fork, surely Joe and Billy wouldn't dare follow?

TRESPASSERS WILL BE PROSECUTED!

Fear propelled his legs, but a stitch began to tear at Alfie's side as he sped along a tree-lined drive. Keeping to the shadows, he darted from one tree to another until he reached the end. There the drive split into two and circled a manicured lawn before meeting again in front of vast steps that led to the front door.

The sky, already coloured with red and gold streaks, was reflected in Atherington Manor's huge windows. Anybody could be in there, looking out at him.

The land was level here, but behind the house the hill began to rise. If he could get around the side of the building unseen, he'd be able to find the ghost road that led straight to the stones.

There was no cover at all. He just had to trust to luck. Taking a deep breath, he cut across the lawn and ran towards the corner of the house. He expected at any moment to hear a shout but he got there without being stopped. Then he crept along the side, keeping close to the wall, bending almost double each time he came to a window.

When he reached the back of Atherington Manor, he discovered there was a paved yard. A large barn and a coach house stood on the far side. Across it, parallel to the back of the manor, were two lines of stables joined by an archway that Alfie guessed marked the start of the ancient route.

He could see it in his mind's eye. The whole village, assembled there in the yard when His Lordship was still alive, holding flaming torches, ready to begin the long walk to the stones.

If he could make it across the yard unnoticed, he could get onto the ghost road then follow it up to the stones and to Smidge.

He listened quietly for a moment. He couldn't hear any signs of life. The kitchen was probably at the back of the house, wasn't it? Yet there were no sounds of pots banging or servants talking to each other. Maybe everyone had gone to the nativity play? He had no idea who worked for Lady Atherington from the church congregation but surely some of them did?

There was nothing for it. He had to take the risk. He started across the open yard towards the archway. He was almost there, the road was in sight, a line of short, sparse grass leading straight uphill, when he heard a shout somewhere behind him.

"Oi! Stop!"

Alfie, naturally obedient, halted. He turned. There was no one there. And then he heard the shout again, angrier this time.

"You two lads! I said *stop!*"

Alfie realized it was coming from the other side of the house. Then there was Joe Copper's voice: "There's a trespasser, Mister. A poacher."

Followed by Billy: "We saw him! He went that way."

Alfie didn't wait to hear more. He fled, wings flapping, sandals slapping on the paving stones, running through the arch towards the ghost road.

He could hear more shouts behind him now. A man, raising the alarm. People calling to each other.

And, the moment his feet hit the sparse grass, he heard other sounds too. A strange, foreign language. Singing, almost. A murmuring that rose and fell like waves on the beach. It was all around him, but he couldn't see anyone. Alfie's flesh prickled into goosebumps. He stopped. Turned around. And the world blurred at the edges, Atherington Manor faded away to nothing and, in its place, a cluster of conical, tent-like shelters emerged as if from mist.

The people who lived in them were taking shape too, translucent to begin with but becoming more solid with each second that passed. They were standing in a circle. As they chanted, they lit flaming torches, one from the other, passing fire around the ring. When the last was alight, the circle broke open and into the middle stepped the old woman.

And Smidge.

It was clear he was captive, and yet wasn't tied up. There was no need for that, Alfie realized: there was nowhere for Smidge to run. The boy hung his head. Defeated.

The old woman raised her arms and the circle rearranged itself into two lines of people, men, women, children, ready to march towards the stones. Like guards. Escorting a prisoner to his execution.

Was Alfie in Smidge's world? Was Smidge in his?

Ancient and modern, both worlds seemed overlaid, one on the other. He could see Smidge's people, but he could hear other voices too, an uproar, a man shouting, "Trespasser!"

And Lady Atherington, snapping back in her high, tight voice, "Get after him!"

Then there were dogs barking and Alfie's chest tightened with fear. A familiar voice – maybe Ted's – shouted, "Don't!"

Alfie didn't stop to think. He pelted towards the two columns of Smidge's people. They couldn't see him. None of them could see him. He started yelling his friend's name.

"Smidge! Smidge!"

And Smidge looked up. "Effie!"

The boy's face, which had looked so beaten with despair a moment before, shone with hope.

"Run, Smidge! Run!" screamed Alfie, grabbing his arm, tugging him along. Smidge didn't hesitate. He sprang forward and the two boys were fleeing, side by side.

Smidge's captors clearly hadn't expected him to escape. When Smidge started running, there was a stunned, horrified silence.

Then a yell of outrage ripped through the air. And someone – Starver, probably – was barking orders. Smidge's people were coming in pursuit.

And in Alfie's world, if it had been Ted who shouted, "Don't!", his plea came too late because the barking became baying. Alfie stumbled and almost fell as he realized with horror that Lady Atherington's dogs had been unleashed and set on him.

*　*　*

As the two boys sprinted along the ghost road, Alfie and Smidge seemed to slip from one world to the other.

One moment they were being pursued by Smidge's people. The road ahead lay clear and straight all the way to the headland. The next, Alfie could hear Billy Figgs and Joe Copper and a whole lot of other children. There were adults' voices too. Trying to stop Billy and Joe? Egging them on? It was impossible to tell.

In Alfie's world, the ghost road was bisected by a lane. He could see the hedge a hundred yards or so ahead. If they could get over that, they'd be off Lady Atherington's land and the dogs would be called back. He and Smidge could run up the lane towards Coombe Farm and safety.

Smidge and Alfie were fast, but Lady Atherington's dogs were much, much faster. Ninety yards to the hedge. Eighty. Alfie could hear the baying getting louder and louder. Seventy. Sixty.

They were close now. He could hear their paws thudding on the grass. Fifty. Forty.

A dog's hot breath was on his calves, but before its teeth could close on Alfie's flesh, he slipped into Smidge's world, where the clan had fanned out. Many were still behind, but some had gone to the right, others to the left, as they had when they'd been hunting.

Yet now, there was the hedge again. Thirty yards away now. Then twenty. Ten.

The confused dogs had lost them, but only momentarily. The barking and the baying began again, more furious than ever.

Nine yards. Eight.

Snapping teeth. A furious, bloodthirsty snarl. The whoosh of air as one of the dogs leapt at Smidge's back … and disappeared before it made contact.

Smidge's people had encircled them. The flaming torches were closing in. Then fading as the boys slipped once more into Alfie's time.

They reached the hedge, both panting. If Alfie could keep Smidge with him now, in 1939, they would be all right as long as Lady Atherington's dogs didn't get them. Before Alfie could even think about how to get over the hedge, it melted away.

They were back in Smidge's world. And time had run out. His people were laying rough hands on him, and Alfie – a ghost of the future – could do nothing. He was invisible here. Ineffectual. Unseen by everyone except Smidge, who cried, "Effie, Effie…!" as they bound his wrists.

Pushing Smidge ahead of them, torches held high, the old ones walked towards the headland and the stones.

MIDWINTER SACRIFICE

Alfie stayed beside Smidge every step of the way, his arm around his friend's shoulders. They leaned their heads together, but whether Alfie was comforting Smidge or Smidge was comforting him, he couldn't say. Alfie couldn't stop the tears streaming down his face and his heart ached so badly he thought he would die. He would almost have welcomed it, he thought. The knowledge of what was to come was unbearable.

It was a dreadful, dreadful journey. Smidge's people had resumed their chanting the moment Smidge was captured. They kept it up all the way to the headland, walking increasingly quickly, pointing at the sky, hurrying to reach the stones before sunset.

The sun was beginning to sink into the sea by the time they arrived, which seemed to alarm the old woman. Hastily, she pointed to various members of the group, uttering names, waving her hand, indicating where each of them should stand. Sinking their flaming torches into the grass at the foot of each of the stones, they took their places. Men held the hands of their children. Women clutched babies to their chests. They all watched silently as the old woman approached Smidge. She took his hands in hers and said something. Soft. Gentle. Heartfelt. Alfie didn't know what the words meant, but it was almost as if she was apologizing for what she was about to do.

Tears spilled out of her eyes and rolled down her face, yet she looked at Starver, and when he offered her the axe that was hanging at his belt, she nodded.

When the old woman walked into the heart of the stone circle and beckoned him in, Smidge gave one last, long look at Alfie then followed her.

"Don't! Smidge, please don't. Don't go!"

Smidge had accepted what was to happen. Alfie hadn't. He stayed by his friend as the old woman turned Smidge around and prepared to administer the fatal blow.

She started chanting, and the others joined in. As the sun sank lower into the sea, she raised the axe. Paused, as if she was waiting for the exact moment when the sun would disappear below the horizon.

The edge of the blade caught the light, flaming blood red.

A stone axe, chipped and sharpened like Smidge's spearhead. The spearhead Alfie still carried in his pocket.

Time slowed. He couldn't be seen in Smidge's world. But Smidge's spearhead surely could. Alfie had no idea what he was doing. Some instinct drove him. Pulling the spearhead from his pocket, he ripped off the handkerchief.

The last sliver of sun was disappearing. The old woman steadied herself.

At the very same moment, Alfie, holding the spearhead high, thrust Smidge aside and stepped forward.

As Smidge fell to the ground, there was a cry of astonishment, a gasp of alarm, a collective, indrawn breath.

Smidge's people were looking at Alfie. They could see him!

A boy with wings, in a white robe, appearing out of thin air, hand raised to stop the axe from falling. Too late.

The axe was already coming down.

And Alfie knew that it would not fall on Smidge,

but on him. Smidge wasn't buried here. He was. The stones had been waiting for him.

Alfie flung his arms wide to receive the blow. He felt the blade bite into his forehead. Into skin.

But not bone.

It passed through the rest of him as if he was made of air.

Because now there were different people, yelling Alfie's name. Searching for him. They were carrying lanterns, because time had slipped out of joint and it was already pitch dark in Alfie's world.

Auntie Bell was calling, "Where are you, my birdie?"

And Ted, "Can you hear me, Alfie?"

Transparent figures, like reflections in glass, Auntie Bell, Ted, Violet, Reverend Braithwaite, Miss Bottomley, all desperately looking for him. All desperately worried. All wishing and hoping and praying that Alfie was safe.

Smidge was still here, and Smidge's people. Yet they were losing definition. Smudging. Blurring.

Had Alfie saved Smidge? Had Smidge saved Alfie? What had happened?

The two boys looked at each other. Smidge's wrists were being unbound by the old woman. There was something in her face that Alfie couldn't recognize.

She didn't seem angry. She looked relieved. Grateful.

Smidge reached a hand out to Alfie and Alfie tried to take it but it was like trying to hold on to water.

Smidge was growing fainter. He transformed from solid to transparent and then to almost nothing at all. Alfie couldn't keep his friend with him.

Time was running like sand through an hourglass. Smidge was a whisper. Then he was gone.

Alfie was entirely in the here and now. A world in which the headland had crumbled and half the stone circle had slid into the sea.

For a fraction of a second, Alfie teetered on the cliff edge.

And then fell.

REDEMPTION

An angel was tumbling into the darkness. Screaming. Falling.

Then thudding into scree. Slithering. Sliding. Wings breaking as Alfie rolled head over heels down the cliff.

He could hear Violet, shouting his name somewhere above. He thought he heard Auntie Bell calling to her to come away from the cliff edge. There was yelling. Crying. Then he heard Ted: "Alfie? Can you hear me, my lad?"

Dazed and aching in both mind and body, Alfie summoned all his strength. He seemed to have stopped falling. But he wasn't in the sea.

"Yes," he called back, voice shaking. "I must be on some sort of ledge, I think."

"Thank the Lord for that. Are you hurt?"

Alfie considered. His head ached and there was something hot and sticky oozing from the cut on his forehead made by the old woman's axe. His arms and legs felt as if he'd been punched over and over again and his wrist was hot and painful as if he'd sprained it. Yet he could still feel his feet and wiggle his toes and just about move his fingers.

"A bit..." he said. "But I don't think anything's broken."

"Right. You stay put. Don't move a muscle. I shall go to the farm directly, fetch some ropes, you hear me? We shall have you out of there in a jiffy."

It took Ted a lot longer than he'd thought. Because of the blackout, all the search party's lanterns were shuttered, and letting out only wafer-thin slivers of light. Ted's journey to the farm and back was difficult, and when he did return, there was the question of how to get Alfie to safety. To be hauled up he'd need to tie a rope around himself, but Alfie could barely feel the fingers on his right hand. Miss Bottomley bravely volunteered to be lowered over the edge, but there was the risk of the cliff crumbling, sending stones hurtling down onto Alfie's head. At night, it really was too dangerous to try. Instead, Auntie Bell made a trip to the farm, bringing back tea and sandwiches and blankets, which were lowered down to Alfie to keep him warm.

Even so, it was a long, long night.

At last, the deep inky black gave way to indigo then turquoise. The rising sun snuffed out the stars. And the moment the sky lightened enough to see a way of getting to Alfie without loosening stones or causing another landslide, Miss Bottomley was lowered over the cliff edge by Ted and Auntie Bell and Reverend Braithwaite. After she'd secured a second rope around Alfie, they were both hauled to safety.

Alfie was exhausted, bruised and in a state of shock. For the second time in only a few weeks he couldn't remember the walk back to the farmhouse. Somehow he was just there, in the warmth of the kitchen, and Auntie Bell was making tea and handing out slabs of cake.

Slowly, Alfie pieced together the events of the afternoon before. It seemed it was Violet who'd raised the alarm. She'd gone running to Auntie Bell, so scared of what Billy and Joe might do she'd persuaded the grown-ups to go after them.

Auntie Bell had been almost out of her mind with worry. So had Violet, who had refused to leave the clifftop until Alfie was safe.

"Why didn't you tell us what was going on, birdie?" said Auntie Bell to Alfie. "You didn't need to be fighting your battles all alone. This is your home. I'm here to look after you. So is Ted. We'd have sorted those lads out if only you'd said."

Alfie didn't know how to reply, but he didn't need to. Auntie Bell seemed to understand how he felt.

While the grown-ups talked about the punishment that would be meted out to Billy and Joe, Violet edged closer to Alfie.

"Billy's in terrible trouble," she said. "He's really going to catch it."

"I thought you were friends with him."

"He didn't give me no choice," she said. "He was always threatening to wallop Jack. But he won't get away with that no more, will he?"

"I suppose not," said Alfie uncertainly.

A silence stretched out between them that was broken by Violet saying suddenly, "You ain't like them others. You're different."

Alfie grunted. "Strange, you mean. Bonkers."

"No, I don't. I mean special."

Alfie examined her face for signs of mockery and saw there was nothing but a silent plea for him to like her. "Thanks," he said gruffly.

And then Violet lowered her voice to a whisper. "Up there – on the cliffs. I thought I saw…"

Alfie's heart skipped a beat. "What?"

"I dunno. They looked like ... ghosts... Cavemen or something."

Alfie didn't say anything.

"I suppose you think I'm barking mad," said Violet with a watery smile.

"No," said Alfie. He was going to say more but it felt too early to talk to her about Smidge. His heart was too sore for that. Maybe when he knew Violet a bit better, trusted her a bit more? Maybe someday he'd confide in her.

Meanwhile, there were cows to be milked and eggs to be collected and it was time to get started. Miss Bottomley and the vicar were yawning their heads off, so, after bidding the children goodbye, they left the farmhouse and headed away to their beds.

Ted was already whistling for the dogs and starting up the lane to bring the herd in.

"Do you really help with milking?" Violet asked.

"Yes," said Alfie.

"You're brave, Alfie Wright. I'd be scared as anything."

"No, you wouldn't," said Alfie. "Not if you got to know the cows. They're soft as butter. Especially Primrose. Want to come and meet her?"

Though her eyes were red-rimmed with weariness, Violet stifled a yawn and smiled. "Yeah. All right."

PART IV

The Seer had been right about Smidge. She should never have doubted it. The reason the boy had repeatedly come to mind was not because the Goddess wanted him sacrificed! No... The Goddess wanted him saved. Mother Earth had known – of course She had – of a Darkness that was growing in the minds of the clan. The Seer had misunderstood.

They had come so close to catastrophe! But then the Goddess had sent that winged creature to save Smidge. A thing of air and light, a creature of the sky, and not from the realm of demons. It offered itself up, took the boy's place. Dissolving into nothing as the axe blade passed through.

There could be no more certain sign of divine favour! The creature had been sent to save Smidge from the clan's misguided folly. They would not doubt again. Even Starver, who had so long whispered against Smidge, was now assured that the child was a blessing and not a curse.

Smidge would live to fulfil his destiny. And the Seer had no doubt whatsoever that his future would be glorious.

REWRITING HISTORY

Christmas came and went. The new year started. They were more than halfway through January when Auntie Bell received a letter from Professor Shaw and Professor Higgins asking if they could stay at Coombe Farm again. It seemed that, on re-examination of the bones, they had discovered they'd made a terrible mistake. It wasn't a *child's* body that had been buried, as they'd first thought, but that of an adult: a man who had lived to a great age and died of perfectly natural causes. They couldn't imagine how they'd made such a fundamental error. They were desperate to have another look at the burial site to see if there was anything else that they'd missed.

They arrived at the end of the month and set straight to work.

Alfie had no idea if the buried bones were Smidge's. The idea of his friend growing up, of becoming an old man, was strange and uncomfortable. But if that wasn't Smidge, what had happened to him? In the last few weeks, little by little, Alfie had told Violet about his friend. Talking to her had helped, but the not knowing still niggled away at him.

And then, one afternoon towards the middle of February, Violet came home with Alfie for tea. They were tucking in to wedges of homemade bread slathered with butter and bramble jelly and listening to Auntie Bell's steady stream of chatter, when the two professors burst through the kitchen door in a state of high excitement.

The old men paid no heed whatsoever to Auntie Bell or the children but simply continued the conversation they'd been having before they came in, talking so fast that not even Auntie Bell could squeeze a word in edgeways.

Alfie couldn't follow a lot of it because they used such long, technical words, though he managed to grasp enough to understand that the man who had been buried at the stones had been an important, highly respected individual. A chieftain, they thought, or a holy man: someone greatly revered by his people. He'd been laid in the ground with enormous care and with a huge hoard of what they called "grave goods": precious things his people would send with him to the afterlife. Axe heads. Spears. Several elaborate necklaces. Similar objects had been discovered before at other burial sites across Europe.

And yet the history books were going to have to be rewritten now, they agreed. Because that very day they had unearthed an extraordinary carving of a human figure. Again, small figurines had occasionally been found at other ancient sites, but this one had wings that made it resemble a modern-day angel. Why, it wouldn't look out of place on the top of a Christmas tree! How could that be? the archaeologists asked each other. It was baffling!

And – more flummoxing still – they had also discovered a circular disc of glass. It was impossible for anyone to have possessed such a thing! The body had been buried hundreds, possibly even thousands of years before anyone was either trading or making glass in Europe. And yet it was there with the other grave goods, and had undoubtedly been buried at the same time. It really was the most peculiar, inexplicable mystery. The two men scratched their heads and looked utterly perplexed.

"If I didn't know better," Professor Shaw told Professor Higgins, shaking his head at the absurdity of the idea, "I'd say it was the lens of a magnifying glass!"

At which point Alfie threw back his head and let out a yelp of triumphant joy.

"Yes!" he said, punching the air. "Yes! I saved him!"

"You did!" Violet shrieked. "You did! You clever thing. Oh, well done, Alfie!"

And suddenly the two children were jumping up and down for sheer joy.

The two professors peered at Alfie and Violet over their spectacles with such comically alarmed expressions on their faces that Auntie Bell began to giggle. So did Alfie. And Violet. Once they'd started, the three of them couldn't seem to stop. They carried on until the tears were streaming down their faces and they were all so weak with laughter they could barely stand.

TANYA LANDMAN is the author of many books for children and young adults. She is best known for her award-winning historical novels for both middle-grade and YA readers, including *Buffalo Soldier*, which won the Carnegie Medal, *One Shot*, which won the Scottish Teenage Book Prize, *The Goldsmith's Daughter*, *Hell and High Water*, *Beyond the Wall* and, most recently, *Horse Boy*. For *Mondays are Murder,* the first in her hugely popular middle-grade murder mystery series, Tanya won the Red House Children's Book Award, which was voted for entirely by children. You can find out more about Tanya and her books by visiting her website: www.tanyalandman.com